PHZED

PHZED

Glenn D. Glasgow

ISBN: 978-1-64713-360-3   (Paperback Edition)
ISBN: 978-1-64713-361-0   (Hardcover Edition)
ISBN: 978-1-64713-347-4   (E-book Edition)

Book Ordering Information

Phone Number: 347-901-4929 or 347-901-4920
Email: info@globalsummithouse.com
Global Summit House
www.globalsummithouse.com

Printed in the United States of America

Rules in the game of life

Anybody for a game of FAZED? asked an overly excited Brin, the paintbrush that stands about nine inches long and is about five inches across at his brush base.

A bolt of lightning followed by a crack of thunder came after Brin said that. It was almost as if a higher power wanted to emphasize what was just said. Brin's once well-crafted handle is white, but some would say it is yellow wood with a light gold metal trim where the brush meets the wood. His brush base is pitch black, well, most of it anyway, at least most of what is left. He has been used so much over the years that some of his hair has fallen out of place, some has even been twisted a little, while others were cut short. He now has wrinkled cracks in some places from all the debris he has had to clear from time to time, and he did mention a few times that it is high time he retired.

"FAZED?" asked Stan. "I'll get the dice."

Once again a flash of lightning and the massive roll of thunder followed. Perhaps a higher power was indeed at play here in response to what Stan just said as well, but Stan is no saint or angel. He is a hammer that is shaped like a geologist's hammer and is roughly about fourteen inches long. His wood top is chipped from the tip to his metal base, and being the only hammer in the garage over the years, the metal head has dents in it indicating where he has pounded so many nails over time

He has a sharply pointed head that he, as well as others who know him and have used him in the past, claims is a radar, one that guides him in the correct direction when he is pounding a nail or chipping away at some hard or ancient rock. He ran off to the red toolbox and grabbed the dice. There he has found refuge and longed for peace in the past.

"We will need six players," said Ed, a blue handled and oversize flathead screwdriver that hangs around and plays with his family in most of his free time. Ed is about eleven inches long and roughly one half of an inch in circumference at the head. For Ed to join the group was a bit unusual. He prefers to spend time with his family and do stuff with them. He has often said, "Time spent with them is like putting money in the bank; you have to invest in it if you want it to grow."

His family is made up of the most extensive amount of members of all the tools. Of late, most of their time now is spent idle. There used to be a time, not too long ago it seems when the owner had a use for all those different screwdrivers, but the times sure have changed. They are lucky if more than one is used in any given month.

"I'll have to have the rest of my family join us to make up the remainder of the players," said Ed.

As is almost always the case, Ed's family again is going to make up for the rest of the team, if not most. The screwdrivers included not only Ed and his wife Phyllis but their kids. They also added two aunts, two uncles, several cousins and all four grandparents. With their vast numbers, once upon a time, they were able to influence much of what happened inside the garage. It had become a common practice to expect to have two or more of them included in every event, whether that be a friendly game, or a building or repair project.

Most of the time, just to keep the family bonding as one, the screwdrivers would go off and do things on their own and not include the other tools in the garage. It is not as if the other devices were not invited, but the screwdrivers tend to stick to themselves and talk about their families, and do things among themselves. They had been doing this for so long that now everyone expects them not to invite outsiders.

Ed's wife, Phyllis, a green-handled Phillips head screwdriver is slightly shorter than her husband by about three inches and is about the same size in circumference. She is almost equal, in influence. She came over and brought a few of the kids, all purple heads, to join with the rest of the players.

This game was one of the few in which the younger screwdriver can participate with the adult tools and not feel out of place. In fact, this was one of the games in which the younger screwdrivers performed very well, if not better than some of the adults. They fared well due to a combination of a few things, such as their vivid and seemingly unlimited imagination, and their constant quest for knowledge; plus, being around the likes of Porter has also helped tremendously.

The other tools in the garage, greatly outnumbered by screwdrivers, tended to cheer each other on during the games whenever permitted. No one dared to argue with Ed or Phyllis as they always seemed to have the home court advantage.

The screwdrivers were a family that played together and stayed together and this family was the envy of the garage.

"This game is best played with six players," said Dae, who in his lifetime has had the dual role of being a mason's trowel and an archaeologist's best friend. He was more than just a favorite old tool in his field. His vast knowledge and diverse talent, as well as his wisdom and function, have been unchanged since his inception.

He was once considered an extension of his archaeologist owner's hand, an owner that has since sold off Dae at a garage sale, where he was picked up by his current owner. While the mason will use this tool to, plaster, level, spread, or shape substances such as cement or mortar, a gardener will most often use its pointed, scoop-shaped blade for digging and setting plants. An archaeologist would merely use it to dig, carry, cut, and sometimes scrape. To the trained archaeologist's ear however, the trowel plays music which it seems only he understands.

By striking an object with a particular intensity, the blade will echo a high-pitched song. The more robust the object it hits the higher-pitched song it relays.

An archeologist can easily predict what is beneath him by listening to this "music."

The other tools were never quite sure of Dae's relatives, history or family tree. After all, he was one of a kind and the only one of his kind in the garage.

In recent memory, no one could recall the last time Dae went outside and did some work. They respected him for his brilliance and based on how everyone would reference him in playful disputes he was apparently the judge or the arbitrator of all the tools. He was also the one everyone looked to whenever there was a tie or a deadlocked vote, or a minor or significant argument or discussion. Dae was not so much a father figure, but more of a grandfather figure, an elder that everyone respected listened to and looked up.

"Dae" is short for Daedal, so nicknamed because in the garage he is the "they" in "that's what they say." His name changed in spelling, but not in pronunciation. Whenever a tool wanted to get a point across, especially in Dae's absent, he could always rely on one of the old familiar phrases: "Well, that's what Dae says," or "that's what Dae said," or "that's what Dae would say," and "that's what Dae would do."

Dae, as his name defines, is ingenious and sophisticated in design as well as function, and he is artistic. None of the tools ever called him Daedal though. For as long as anyone can recall he has always been known merely as Dae.

Like most of the tools in the garage, he was now aging some. His wooden handle is not only darkened now but slightly chipped in more than one spot. His once shiny stainless steel surface now has a few places that are showing some rust and some bending along the sides.

The game got its name from the mispronunciation and misspelling of it by none other than Porter. Porter, the nail gun, who when he was introduced to the other tools, claimed to have grown up on the streets in the wrong neighborhood. He also claimed that he has spent the better part of his adolescent life jumping from pawn shop to pawn shop through several different owners. He came into the lives of the other tools here with a unique way of taking a word and changing its spelling, most of the time to the point that few if anyone of the other tools could understand. Often he would give new meaning to words that all the tools were familiar with. For example, Porter has more than once referred to their home, the garage, as the "case." Those who did understand him spent a lot of time listening and conversing with him to get to the point. The others had to have things repeated and explained to them in the hope that one day they would understand without having what he just said translated.

Most of the tools did come to a general understanding that Porter's slang, as well as his unique way of changing words, were excellent for their everyday conversation. But they agreed that he could not use them in this particular game, mainly when he wanted to create a new word along the way. The general rule of thumb was everyone had to use Standard English words so that everyone else could understand. Porter was one of the last of the old tools to join the crowd. He was so unique, they tolerated his street talk as a way to make him feel more welcome and not like such an outcast, because no other tool did what he did, or said what he said. His sheer strength and drive were what most of the other devices particularly admired, but his massive size always gave him a complex, a feeling of inferiority that perhaps he was mentally slow. All the other tools could fit neatly on a peg hook on the wall, but not Porter, he had to be placed on the countertop or somewhere else where he could take up all the space he needed. Porter was also the only tool that required the assistance of an air compressor to get his job done, or at least to keep him energized.

Sometimes when he was in use, his long air cord stretched out so far it wrapped around several times in a circle and created a mini mountain in the middle of the floor. When not in use, this cord was detached and wrapped around the compressor at the head.

Although Porter and the compressor, along with its cord came into the garage at the same time, the three of them never really were together. The compressor and its cord pretty much stayed together while Porter went to work or wandered off into his own little world.

It's widely believed that neither one or the other, the compressor nor its cord, actually wanted to be around Porter anyway, and Porter felt the same way about them. Although Porter relied on his compressor for all of his strength, everyone quickly learned that the two, when not in use, did not spend any time together, as the screwdrivers did. In fact, Porter distanced himself from the compressor, as did all of the other tools for that matter.

Even the screwdrivers avoided the compressor. Perhaps because it was too loud, or maybe it would kick up too much dust every now and again, or take a vast amount of electricity to run it. Whenever it was turned on, the rumble from it would shake the walls, and make the place feel like an earthquake was passing. Another reason could be when it was turned on, it was so loud the neighbors could hear it and someone once said, "tools should be seen and not heard." Most of the compressor's time was spent away from view, and no one not even Dae it seems made an effort to include it in anything the group was participating in.

The great thing about this game is you never know where it is going to lead you, or where you are going to end up, or what you are going to end up as. You have to go with the flow and try to keep up with it wherever it may take you.

Before Porter came along, the game was called merely "PHASE," but Porter was able to convince the group to change the spelling of it. He claimed that the old spelling was too outdated. Where as on the streets a "PH" sounding word was more "hip" at least in his circles and so more in keeping with the times. He suggested they should keep it, but he then insisted that "ASE" should change because it did not go with anything. So to keep up with the times (most of the tools wanted to feel young and be somewhat hip with pop culture) thename was changed. But this was done only after a brief discussion with the other elder devices and lots of peer pressure. They decided they should go with what Porter suggested. At least for now, the younger generation wanted it so.

Porter said that the "ASE" had a somewhat "AZE" sound to it, as he liked the British pronunciation of the letter "Z" as opposed to the American pronunciation of it. So instead of saying "AZE" as in the United States, he pronounced the letter "Z" as "zed."

So the game got its new name. At first, some of the elders could not get used to the new name or its pronunciation, so they called it "FA-ZED." With so many of the young screwdrivers around to remind the elders of its pronunciation, its name changed to its new spelling: "PHZED."

Pretty much all the screwdrivers' kids and the other young tools could understand Porter and converse with him without pause, making Porter happy. They all accepted the change even though they all did not agree with the way it was to be pronounced. By accepting it, they were able to maintain their sense of family or at least togetherness.

Porter one day got tired of the adults telling him his manner of speaking was not correct and how it made him sound unintelligent to others. That touched off a firestorm. An irate Porter countered with a little history lesson that put their criticism of his language to rest forever. That very day and in a furious tone, Portor started talking.

"Did you know that English started in what is now the western part of Germany?" Porter said to the tools. It was spoken by the Saxons and the Angles, two minority groups in old Germany. Just like minority groups here in America, it was their unique language that distinguished their speech from the rest of the general population." No one seemed particularly impressed and or convinced, but they were giving him their undivided attention.

"English," he went on to say, "is made up of not just one language, but many different languages, that continue to grow to this day. We use words, many of these words that are not English in origin at all."

The other tools were now appearing to be very impressed, although at first, they did not believe him. But after some quick research, they saw that Porter was indeed correct and that put an end to their comments about the way he spoke. Plus, they became aware that English had a family tree that dated back centuries, from the Anglo-Saxon to Old English, to Middle English, to Modern English. It included phrases that someone of today's generation, looking back at old English, would have a tough time comprehending. The one thing about the English history lesson is that just like this game, it also shows that no matter how remote or unlikely the possibilities are, we're all connected to each other in some way.

To select the players for the game and to get the order in which they were to play, each player would start by rolling the dice once. Whatever number the dice landed on would be that player's assigned number. Since there were six players this time, each would have an assigned number one through six.

Once you rolled the dice and got a number (unless you got one already in use) you could not re-roll the dice to get a different number, even if you wanted your "lucky" number. If a player got a number already taken, then he or she must roll again and again until he or she got a unique number and all six numbers on the dice were taken. Players could play as individuals or on a team. If you were on a team, you could not pre-select your teammate. For those players who chose to have teammates, the opposite number on the dice would be that of their partner, and they could not change it.

So, for example, if someone got the number six, his or her partner was the number one, and if someone got the number three, his or her partner's number is four, and so forth. This is because the opposite sides of a dice always add up to seven. This is done so no one can select or predict who his or her teammate will be. Each player will get to play with someone he or she would not normally play with or sit next to if he or she had the choice. It gave everyone the chance to have to integrate with someone new each time. For this game, the six players were now selected and seated in a circle. They included Brin, Dae, Ed, his wife Phyllis, Porter, and Stan.

In an unusual coincidence, Ed and Phyllis sat next to each other, and seated directly behind them were three of their kids and four other relatives (although they were not part of the game, just there for support). The tool with the highest number, 6, starts the game.

Phzed is sometimes played with as few as four players, although it has been known to be played a few times with just two or three.

Player one selects a two or three-word combination, or a person's name which could include the first, middle (or middle initial) and last name and says it out loud. Whoever is starting the game (as in this case, the one with the number six) when selecting a name or phrase must choose a phrase or name that contains precisely six letters. In other words, the first, second and third word must include just six letters because this player rolling is the number six.

This has often been an issue for some of the players and since the player going first has the highest number, he or she is allowed to use the dictionary or a thesaurus to find the first-word name or a combination of three words to start the game. Player one, however, is the only one allowed to use the dictionary or any other outside source the entire duration of the game and it is only to get the game started. Once the name or phrase is said out loud, the one to the right or left of that player has a time limit to respond with a link word or phrase to a part of that name or part of the sentence. The time limit for each response is also predetermined before the game is to begin.

An independent person is selected to keep track of the time, even though players could quickly do it for themselves. That independent person is there to free up the players' minds, so they do not have to think of their time limit. They can concentrate on the game. When there are not enough players available to allow for an independent timekeeper, the player passing the baton onto the next player is ultimately responsible for the timekeeping. This time limit is determined by whoever was the last to roll the dice, and their number is multiplied by two. That number becomes the number of seconds one has to respond to the player before them.

So, for example, if the last player to roll the dice gets number five, then the time limit to respond is ten seconds. The player with the highest number and the one who rolls last are the only two with any special privileges. The player who starts the game also can determine which direction the game is to go, whether it is to the left or the right, and the entire game is played in this direction.

With confirmation that all the rules are clear to all the players, the game begins. The first name or phrase selected was the phrase, "London Bridge," two words, each containing six letters.

The one next to him or her, player two, has 12 seconds to respond with a name or phrase that has either the word "London" or "Bridge," in it to continue. Player two can link one of the words in any form, as long as it contains a two or three-part name or phrase. The next player may say something to the effect of, "London fog," "bridge the gap," "Bridge-Romme," or "London Eye." Then it is passed onto player three who now has 12 seconds to respond to that with another link, and the game continues to the next person to the right or left, etc., etc., etc.

Since you can work in teams, if you are number five, your partner is number two. Then he or she can answer in your place if you should stumble and cannot come up with a link in the 12 seconds to continue the game. If you should pass it on to your partner, the time limit is by default six seconds, but it starts over with you passing it to your partner. When your partner takes it from you, even if he or she could not link anything at that point, he or she can pass it back to you to continue as long as the time limit has not expired. The time limit restarts only on the first pass to your partner. So if you cannot link a word and you pass it on, and your partner stumbles as well but then you think of a link, he or she can pass it back to you as long as it is still within the time limit. If that player correctly links part of the name or phrase, he, she or their team collect 100 points. If either teammate cannot connect the name or phrase, then they must say, "pass", and the chance is passed onto the next player to the right or left.

A player can say "pass" only three times during the game, but by saying "pass", you lose 25 points each time for you and your two-member team. If one player quits, all of his or her points are given to the partner. A player can excuse himself or herself to go and do something else. Players can excuse themselves for no given reason whatsoever and have all of their points offered to their partners. If one player is eliminated, the partner will still be left in the game to carry on, until that partner's removed. Players are eliminated by points being taken away by saying "pass" and running into deficits that reach100. Anyone can change the phrase or name at any given time, just as long as it contains part of the phrase or name of the given phrase or name. The last one standing, which is usually the one with the most points, wins the game.

This game was played until it was just Dae and Ed remaining. Even though Ed had his wife Phyllis as his teammate, Dae still had more than twice as many points as they did combined. Now it was Dae's turn to connect the phrase passed on to him from Ed. Sometimes, though, for the sake of time, or if Sam or his wife came in and interrupted by taking one of the tools away for a mini-project, then the players would usually agree to end the game and declare the one with the most points the winner, as they did in this case. This time, Sam or his wife did not interrupt this game. Ed wanted to leave and go out and do something else with his wife, which to him usually comes first, so he was more than willing to give up trying to win and instead go and spend the time with his family.

On this particular day, Dae started and won the game, as he has done so many times before. When the tools play any other game that does not involve thinking, perhaps something physical, and there is a winner other than Dae, the winner usually erupts in celebration. The celebration could include loud cheering and hand clapping, but this is never the case with Dae. With another victory under his belt, Dae stretched his arms up and out as if to say without words that he was tired, tired of always winning. But with his class and restraint, he did not even so much as smile. He merely shook the hands of Ed and Phyllis and said, 'excellent job, excellent work,' and patted them on the back as they moved on.

MEETING THE NEW TOOLS

"**S**ometimes I like to think of all the things I could have done, and all I should have done," said Dae from out of nowhere, and it did not appear that he was speaking to anyone in particular.

The game was now long over, and with nothing else to do, all of the players who were eliminated or withdrew just sat around to watch the game come to an end. There is always the chance, they think, and that they will miss an opportunity to learn something if they should leave, so they all stayed. It has become almost a ritual to see Dae move with such grace when he wins at thinking games.

"The worst thing a man can do in his life is not doing the one thing he is afraid of doing. The worst thing a soldier can do is not to fight the fight he was trained to do," Dae said, as he sat in the same spot where he was playing the game, looking down at his shadow.

Dae thinks that the other tools see him as a long-forgotten garden shovel, one that once was shiny and new and worked everyday like the original and fancy electronic tools that now cling to the wall of the garage.

It was not too long ago that Sam's wife had a garden outside the house where she planted roses and grew some organic vegetables. This was her passion, and in his heyday, Dae was her tool of choice. She has long since decided to let go of this passion and allow her husband to build a deck on the site where the once thriving garden was. It was her pride and joy and the envy of the neighbors.

Dae was now showing some signs of aging as well, with the tip of his base slightly rusted. He now sports a chipped wooden handle, indented with a handprint, showing where he was held time and time again by those who worked with him over the years. Dae was the primary tool used in this once flourishing garden. He has watched tomatoes grow from seeds to full blooming stalks and roses that were once little green stems which have long since blossomed into bright red, pink and white flowers that were given away to friends, family, from well-wishers usually on special occasions. It saddens him to think that everything he has worked so hard and long for now was destroyed to make way for someone else's passion. He seems sad sitting there, looking down at his shadow with his hands open, looking at his palms, knowing that he could not do anything about the garden he has watched from birth.

Inside the garage, it is like it has been on most days, except this was a Saturday, an ordinarily calm Saturday morning on the inside, but outside, that is an entirely different story.

A massive hurricane was passing over the city, and the imposed mandatory curfew meant everyone had to stay indoors, at least until the storm had passed. With the electricity cutting in and out, radio or television was out of the question. There was no telling what might happen if these tools were taken outside. The weatherman was correct; this storm had slowed down considerably since it had entered the city. That also meant that Sam, the owner of the house where the garage and tools live, could not work on the deck he planned to build this weekend, which was on the spot where his wife's garden once stood. He was energized all week to do it this weekend, he did not want to think that the weatherman would be right. Unfortunately the weather report was correct. The storm shifted and came directly towards the city, so his plans had to change as well.

The weatherman did say that this was a storm unlike any other before it. This hurricane was going to be a big slow-moving storm and its effect would last for more than one day and could cause massive damage and flooding throughout the area. With such a warning, almost everyone took the usual precautions and boarded up their houses and stocked up on supplies for themselves, their family and their pets, in preparation for an extended period without any electricity, and perhaps clean water. The dog and the cat were both brought inside the house, for their safety. The owner's cat spent most of his time indoors on the sofa anyway, and there was a small cutout in the doorway where he could come and go as he chose when needed. The dog, however, pretty much stayed outside in his secure doghouse.

For the first time, from what most of the tools recall, the car was brought into the garage. Most of the time, its night was spent outside in the driveway. The car did not take up all of the garage space, however. After all, this was a two-car garage, and the car mostly occupied one side of the garage, with the tools and some other miscellaneous items on the other wall, the wall facing the sunrise. With the garage attached to the main house, Sam could still walk in and out of it as he chose which is what he did once again to check out his two new tools.

The other tools were unaware that they had new members of the family joining them. All they could see was this new box on top of the counter that no one paid any attention to, in fact, no one even noticed that this unmarked box was there until Sam came in and opened up the box and took out his two new toys.

"There you are," said a smiling Sam, clapping his hands. "There are my babies." One at a time he took out the new tools and then the other device and placed them on top of the counter, his eyes wide open, only his smile was more full.

It was a new cordless drill, red with blue and red paint along its side.

It had 24 volts of power and the ability to run for hours on end without having to recharge its battery. This new drill had 25 different clutch positions for him to use, depending on the job at hand. It was unlike the old one with only ten. With its larger, bolder and more accessible design and more comfortable grip, it was a tool that even Sam's wife could use. Yes, this new cordless drill was more user-friendly and appears designed with the modern do it yourself woman in mind.

He bought this one because he was tired of his previous drill continually stripping screws. His wife suggested that it was not so much the drill's fault but more of a drill bit issue. Sam still insisted on getting a new drill. With its attached cord, the old drill limited where and how far he could go while working with a long extension cord. He held the new drill up in the air for a while, turning it around looking at its different parts, reading the sides and watching it. Perhaps he expected to see or learn something new. He removed the battery and then reattached it, but he did not turn it on. He then placed it down on the counter.

Yes, Sam was like a kid with a new toy. He just had to play with it a few more times, just to be sure it was real and he was not dreaming. He smiled with satisfaction then steered his attention to the other new tool, his new cordless saw. This saw was black and red all over, could operate at speeds of 2000 strokes per minute. With its 2.6 amp volts battery, it could easily trim down 100 two-by-four pieces of lumber in no time flat.

This was unprecedented power. This new saw took the place of Sam's old hand saw, which would take several minutes of cutting back and forth by hand to reduce a simple two-by-four. This new tool could do that same job in seconds.

It was a showpiece, with its incredible ability to cut in any direction, even upside down, and to cut through not just wood and some metals, but also drywall.

The things that would take Sam hours to do before, such as cutting pipes, which would require him taking them to the hardware store to have them cut down to his exact specifications, so a simple job took several hours to complete.

He hated the fact that he made multiple trips to the store, which was not only tiring, but the gas involved in driving back and forth was expensive too.

Yes, he was doing as some people do when they have a brand new car parked inside the garage. He found a reason to go and check on it one more time, just in case. Checking in on these new tools was the same as having to pinch himself for a reality check, just to see if his dreams of new tool ownership did come through. This was the first time Sam had opened both tools and brought them out into the open.

Sam paused, and like that kid with the shiny new toy, he turned around again to look at his new tools and walked back over to them. He picked them up again and then put them down on the counter, but this time he placed a new battery in both of them, just to try out the two.

There was silence throughout the garage as all the tools stared at the new tool that they had never heard a word from before.

Sam, holding both tools, one in each arm with his finger on their start buttons, pressed firmly, the new saw and then the new drill came on, with the touch of a button.

Like a large motorcycle that is way too loud for a quiet neighborhood, their rumble and fancy flashing lights were impressive. Never before had any of the other tools in the garage seen or heard anything sounding like this.

A tool not plugged into an outlet still can make a sound and do the same job, perhaps a better one than the one that was plugged in. This was revolutionary! Phyllis could not help but ask out loud, "Does this mean that these new guys will be replacing the old folks in here? "I am way too young to be retired."

"It is the price we pay for progress. Out with the old, and in with the new," said Dae.

"You are not the sharpest tool in here," said Porter to Phyllis. "What do you think, Sam is going to buy fancy new tools that are smaller, more powerful, can perform more tasks, operate at different speeds, and still keep the old ones here? This is not a museum. I will bet he will eventually get tired of these tools taking up all this precious space and take them down to the pawn shop, Goodwill, or have a garage sale just to get rid of them."

Sam's wife had been on his case for some time now to get rid of what she calls his junk and clean up the place for a change. But with Sam now promising to build the deck where her garden once stood, she was more than willing to let him keep the accumulating mess, as she puts it, in the garage at least for now.

He hesitated for a moment before placing them on top of the shelf with the other tools that had adorned his wall which he collected over the years.

To him, it was as if he were placing his dirty laundry in with the clean. Perhaps he did not want them to be contaminated in some way.

The new drill and saw came in the same broad box. This was a bundled set (on sale at the home improvement store) that he could not resist. It was like his wife going into a shoe store and buying a new pair of shoes, because it was at the right price, and she thought it would be a great addition to her wardrobe. He could not pass on this incredible set.

It was not as though his old tools had stopped working; they worked fine. These were just improvements over the old ones, he claimed. Once he got these new tools, he promised his wife; the prior devices would no longer be lying around idle and collecting dust; he would either donate them or have a garage sale.

Sam realized that he had to put these new tools down at least for a bit and go and do something more productive.

Sam then reached for Stan. Stan could not believe what was happening to him. It had been a while since Sam reached for him, a while since he did some work. Ever since Sam had gotten Porter, Stan had been pretty much dormant. Sam had not used him for over a year. Stan once complained that he was sitting around getting old, fat and collecting dust. There was one occasion, however, only a few months back, when Sam's wife bought some stones at the local garden and flower shop to use in her garden. That was in the days when she was working in her garden. She was trying to pound these stones into place. That was the only time in recent memory he could recall getting something to do, but that was Sam's wife, not Sam.

As Sam grabbed Stan, Porter turned to Stan and asked sarcastically, "Do you remember what you are doing?"

"Don't worry," an excited Stan replied, "I'll be back in a flash." He was very eager to show Sam that he still had some life in him and he always knew his stuff.

"It's like riding a bike; once you learn, you can always get better with practice."

"Don't be so overconfident. I know that you are the kind of person who goes away for the weekend but packs for a week," said Ed.

Sam held Stan in one hand, and had a brand new and shiny oversize hook in the other, a hook with a nailhead on its top.

This was the kind of hook he was going to use to hang his new tool on the wall.

Perhaps it was the excitement or the sudden rush of adrenaline he felt, or the overconfidence he had of thinking he always knew what he was doing, but whatever it was, Stan did forget. Sam lifted him up in the air with one hand and used the other hand to hold the hook. On the drive down, Stan missed the nailhead and drove a hole into the wall instead, barely missing Sam's hand in the process.

The other tools on the wall gasped in shock at what they had just witnessed.

Sam, very quick to get frustrated, placed Stan back on the countertop in a hurry not even giving him another chance. Sam made a fist and slammed it down hard onto the counter.

The force by which Sam slammed his hand down made the tools jump. They rose off the counter slightly and came back down again.

Stan frustrated and not being able to do what he wanted to do, stood on the countertop saddened by what had just happened to him. All of his excitement went away very rapidly.

Sam, and not having a clear head right now without comment or thinking what he was doing, grabbed Porter, the nail gun instead. He wanted to finish the job. But the power was out due to the storm, so Porter was not of any use to Sam either.

Sam did not get upset with Porter as he had with Stan. He gently placed Porter back down and turned his attention to the old corded saw and drill. Sam took his corded electrical drill, wrapped the cord around it along with the old saw with its long cord and placed them both in a box in a corner.

Sam gave up trying to put a hole in the wall at least for today. Instead, he took out the new cordless drill and the new cordless saw and placed them in the spot on the wall where the old drill and saw had been.

The tools looked on in horror. Although they could see and knew that the devices placed into the box were being retired and replaced with a newer, stronger and younger set, none of them could believe what was indeed happening. It seemed like it was yesterday that they all came to live here. These tools were still in excellent working condition. Dae once said they were seasoned, not outdated.

The questions ranged from, "what did they do wrong?" to "what had changed? What was new? and "How could they be of no use to Sam anymore?" These were questions that not even Dae could answer, and these were the questions the tools asked of themselves.

Except for the visible signs of wear and tear, and the occasional miss like the Stan incident, there was nothing wrong operationally with these tools. There was a sad look not only on the old tools as they were put away and replaced with the new and vibrant multi-speed tools but also on the old tools remaining on the countertop. It was more than a look; it was a realization that showed that they had indeed come to the end of an era. The world had changed, and everything that was old and outdated had to change as well.

"This is the sad reality of our culture," said Dae. "When you stop performing up to par or make a simple mistake, you are not the way you use to be and everyone wants to replace you with something else." Sam, turned on the new drill and saw, and waved them in the air for a while. Then he turned off the tools and, smiling with satisfaction, placed them back on the wall. He turned around and left the garage, apparently satisfied. But before Sam walked out the door, he looked at the tools on the wall and commented aloud, "As soon as the storm passes, I am gonna take you guys outside, and we are gonna build us one great deck."

When Sam turned them on and off in front of the other tools, it was as if he wanted the other tools to see their glory and yes, they were impressed. The game the tools had played was on the floor. Dae walked over to it and folded it up and placed it in the red toolbox where all the other non-essential tools were kept. The air was so thick inside the garage from the silence that only the sound of the crackling thunder outside could slice it. There was a somber moment as the tools sat there, some sad for the other tools that were retiring, while others sat in fear of the unknown. Just what new tool will come next if Sam should walk back in? What would it be capable of doing?

After putting away the game, Dae thought it was time to end what he thought was the fear and suspicion of the new tools. He stood on the floor and coughed to clear his throat. Usually when he does this, it is to get everyone's attention. "Listen up, everyone," he said, and they all stopped what they were doing and looked in the direction of Dae. Even the two new tools that were brought in paid attention.

Facing the old tools, he said, "Let us move beyond fear and suspicion, let us be mature and take the first step and go over and welcome the new addition to our household. It is our civic duty to go and introduce ourselves to them, and not wait for them to come to us, so let's get off our high horse and walk over single file and make their acquaintance," said Dae. He clapped his hands twice as if to say hurry, or right now. As he said this, he also gestured for them to come closer to him. Dae took the lead and started walking over to the new arrivals as the other tools followed behind him. Although not necessarily in a mad rush, despite Dae's request for a single file, they all clustered around making their way over to the two new additions to their family. As they approached the new tools, the ohhhhh's and ahhhh's coming from them was in unison.

Never before had they seen a tool work so well without some cord attached. These tools did not make the owner do all the work including holding it and using a lot of energy to get to the end of the project, as is the case of such tools like Stan, and Ed the screwdriver. It was difficult to trust this new tool, so they approached with caution.

As they stood in front of the drill, he suddenly came on with a loud voice and yelled, "Boo!" The other tools jumped back, a little shaken. It was the feeling that they got only around Halloween time. Although Dae stood still, he looked at the drill, and the saw and they looked back at him. They realized that he was neither scared or in the mood to play with them. But they presumed he was not angry, and everything was okay.

The drill laughed out loud, proud of himself and the fact that he had successfully not only scared the living daylights out of the old tools, but he had also attained their attention. "Its okay," said the smiling drill, as he is using his hand to gesture for them to come forward and closer to him. One by one they leaned forward, looking at each other, but again they approached with caution.

"Hi, my name is Ed," said the screwdriver to the drill. "And those are the rest of my family," he said pointing to the wall where at least a dozen other screwdrivers stood. This drill was different in his design; the handle where the operator held and activate it had indents where each finger was placed. Each indent provided a soft grip; it fit like a glove. It was the first time an ergonomically designed tool was placed in their midst, and it generated a lot of attention. This was a tool that when Sam was holding it, his hands would not fall asleep or get numb as they did with some of the other tools.

"Nice to meet you as well," said the drill. "My name is Walt, and this here is my cousin Roybe. The two of us have been living together now for over a year, but our family was not always together. Our relatives are mostly sold individually, as were we for a while. One day the manufacturer decided since it was so close to Christmas he needed to move some of us out faster, so those of us that in some way complemented each other were placed together in one set. There was a successful trial period, and now we are the result," Walt continued.

"Nice to meet you both," said Ed, as he began to introduce the tools. "These other guys here are Brin, who has been with us for quite some time; Stan, about the same time as Brin; and Porter, who has been with us since last year, and of course Dae, who has been here the longest," said Ed, as he pointed out the other tools to Walt and Roybe.

"Well it is certainly great to meet all of you," said Walt. "Isn't it, Roybe? He looked at Roybe, who nodded in agreement. Up to this point, it appeared Walt had done most of the talking, while Roybe simply just nodded and shook his head in agreeing and or disagreeing with Walt.

Dae, who has not said a word to the new tools, asked if they would like to play a game of Phzed with the rest of them. (This he said after he had already put away the game). "This way, I think we will get to know you guys a little better as well as letting you get to know us a little better, in a more relaxed atmosphere."

Both Walt and Roybe nodded their heads and said, "Yes they would." This time the game was played with most of the same tools as earlier, except for the two screwdrivers, Ed and his wife Phyllis. None of the other screwdrivers, participated either. Instead, they stood by and just watched and cheered on every player, not taking sides. Dae went on to tell them that they might get a chance to be partners as he explained the game to them. Secretly, Dae did not want them to be partners. He wanted them to be separated so they could get to know other members of their new family, as opposed to just sticking to themselves as they always had done, and as the screwdrivers like to do.

They played for about 30 minutes and made it a lot of fun, even though the two did not get the chance to be partners as they may have wanted to be, they learned the strengths and weakness of their new family. With topics and phrases ranging from religious figures like Pope John Paul to John Lennon, somewhere along the way they ended up with glass houses and once again, Dae become the winner. Ed explained to Walt and Roybe that this is always the outcome, every time they played this game. Although they appeared to take the loss in stride, it was a bitter pill to swallow. Since it was their first time playing this, they had wanted to make a good first impression. This was accomplished without them even being aware of it.

"Well, we will get him the next time around," said Walt, as he and Roybe patted each other on their backs, smiling.

MOVING BEYOND THE GARAGE

The thunder, lightning, and wind were getting stronger outside. Electricity still was continually flickering as if trying to come on every once in a while. Porter, accompanied by all the young screwdrivers wanted to do something other than play another game. He always seemed to get things to go his way. Everyone was tired of playing a game where Dae was the winner, it was apparent that this time would be no different, no matter what that new game would be.

Although the kids often took part in the adult games like PHZED, the adults would never take part in the games the kids were playing by themselves, or with Porter. Porter and the kids were sitting around having conversations by themselves, but they wanted to invite the adults to talk about all the things they wanted to build, dreamed of building, or had created. Porter and his peeps as he often called his fellow tools did not want to do this with only the screwdriver kids, but with everyone sharing their stories. Porter wanted to know where the new tools were coming from, that way he could get a better understanding of their personalities and their likes and dislikes.

Even though everyone seemed to agree that this was indeed a fun and exciting thing to do, no one, jumped up to start talking. There was an uncomfortable silence. Usually, Dae is one of the most vocal supporters of therapy. After a brief pause, Walt raised his hand and stood up to speak. Walt was the first tool in the garage to come equipped with a memory chip and a blueprint of sorts that tells his operator how much torque or pressure he needs to use on specific jobs. Walt did this automatically; he also adjusted his speed, depending on what he was cutting. Although he has not done a lot of building in his short lifetime, his built-in chip enables him to know what he can do and what he will need and how long it will take to accomplish the task at hand.

Walt cleared his throat, cracked his knuckles and began to speak. "Ever since I came about, people have been using me to build everything from skyscrapers to dog houses," said Walt. "I can recall one time recently, when my master came to me. He wanted to build an entire treehouse. It was one of my proudest moments. So much pressure was placed on me. I accepted, met, and exceeded the challenge head-on. I was the only tool he used and most of the time, I am the only tool anyone will ever need," he said placing his hands on his chest.

"It used to be one would need months and an entire array of tools and heavy equipment to get a particular job done. But now, everything is wireless. People want their tools with no strings attached, and that's where I come in. I fill that void," said Walt.

Porter in an unusual move said, "Lordy, I used to be like you and your way of thinking. Every roofer and home builder used me for most of their work. I cannot think of a time or of another tool being used to hold down a roof, like this roof during a storm." He continued. "Before I came along, they would spend hours using a tool like Stan there to drive these nails into the roofs, and there was no guarantee that these nails would hold. When I came along, I was able to apply the correct amount of pressure to get the job done right the first time around."

Ed nodded his head while holding his chin and said, "You know, you are right, but I am thinking here and asking myself, surely there must have been a way to accomplish that task before you got here. There had to be a way to drive a nail into wood and build houses before you or Walt came along."

"Well said," said Dae, "There is a way to get anything accomplished. Even when you are without any resources, someone will think of and find a way, they always do."

After Walt and Porter, no one else was really up for telling his story to the crowd. It was a new thing for the new tools, this openness, and the outpouring of the truth about oneself.

"Lordy, I like this. This is like being on Oprah, or going to confession," said Porter.

In the past, whenever the tools would get tired of playing phzed, they usually would sleep or listen to Dae tell one of his stories, as he was the one member of the group who did most if not all of the talking whenever there was too much silence. Whether it was one of his now famous quotes or just words to live by, one could always rely on Dae to have an answer, or at least lead them in the right direction to find the solution.

"Lordy, you know I just thought that we should talk about the things we do or have done, rather than play a game where the winner is always the same person," said Porter. "But if no one wants to participate, then we could always go back to playing something where the winner is always the same." There was general agreement that they all wanted to do something different other than play Phzed. Ed thought they should walk over to where the retired tools were in the box in the corner and include them in the game as well. So together they all did what Porter suggested.

"Okay, who wants to go now?" asked Walt. Several hands went up, including that of Dae. "Okay we all can't go first, so let's roll a dice, but this time the one with the lowest digit wins," said Porter.

"Yes, yes" was the grumble to this solution. Ed ran and got the dice. They rolled one by one to selected their number. Dae, the third one to roll after Ed and Porter, got number one. Porter yelled out laughing, 'Lordy, this cannot be happening," he said putting both of his hands on his head. "Dae once again, you're number one!" Everyone got a chuckle out of that very expected outcome, but no one cared that Dae was number one. They knew whoever followed Dae had to impress the audience.

Having all the tools' attention is where Dae likes to be. He craves the spotlight, in part because he has a way of getting the other tools' attention with his always on the mark and timely quotes. Although they sometimes do not understand what he means, it is usually in accordance to what they are doing or saying. Standing or sitting shoulder to shoulder, they stared at Dae. Some had their hands folded, while others placed their hands on the shoulder of the one next to them as if they were awaiting instructions on a new assignment. Others just put their hands behind their backs. No one uttered a word as is usually the case when Dae has the floor. With his eyes closed, he slowly descended to the floor and was seated with his legs folded like an "X" into each other. Still, with his eyes closed, he held his hands out in front of him, palms facing down, and slowly lowered them to gesture for everyone who was still standing to sit, but not necessarily in the same position as he did with his legs crossed. Dae gestured for everyone to sit in a circle, that way, they all can get an unobstructed view. The circle had to be rearranged a few times to accommodate everyone, as their repositioning changed its size.

Finally they seated, although not a perfect circle. Everyone sat in complete silence all looking at Dae. Dae with his eyes still closed, smiled before he slowly opened them to the group. This was a new game. Never before was there any discussion of their past or what they had done. They never had a chance to sit in a circle to talk about anything. For the new tools it was also something new. Why they agreed to do it was somewhat of a mystery to the new tools. Perhaps it was the strange and unusual weather outside, or maybe it was a full moon, or even like playing Phzed. You never know what you will find out and how far you will go. No one could say for sure. Even the rules were not clear, but they all knew that if they sat there and listened to Dae, it would all make sense in a bit. Porter and Walt had already said what they wanted to say. No one else was joining in at that time. They just wanted to sit there and listen to Dae from this point on.

"Come, join me now and close your eyes," said Dae, with his eyes now open and looking directly at the group. "I want to take you all to a place long, long, long ago and yes far, far away and tell you of the greatest mysteries ever told, and about the greatest places we're told," said Dae.

"Oh boy, this is gonna be fun," said Ed. "Hold on, let me get the rest of my family to come over here." As he got up, he whistled for the other screwdrivers to come and join him. He hissed by putting his hands in his mouth and blowing as he usually did. All the different screwdrivers, sixteen all together, with smiles on their faces flocked around him, the eight blue flatheads and eight green Phillips expanded the circle even further. Some of them were so small in height that even if they were to stand upright, they were not much taller than the adult tools sitting in the circle.

Walt and Roybe sat there next to each other with an empty look on their faces and showing no particular emotions. Where they come from, there are no tools with that many family members in it. Their family was composed of just one or two of them, so the screwdriver's family took them by surprise. Walt and Roybe were also unaware that Dae was about to tell them one of these stories. In his unique way, he takes them to the place where only their imaginations can go. With the hurricane still going on outside, no one was going anywhere any time soon, so an excellent short story was as good as a movie or a home project or a makeover show on TV.

"Okay let's close our eyes," said Ed. "Close our eyes," he repeated to the rest of his family.

Dae in his storytelling, usually takes on the characters in the story. For example, if it were his great, great, great, grandfather he was talking about, he would tell the story as if he were his grandfather telling it. He would use words like "I" and "we" for emphasis. While telling it, if one of the characters had to cry, he was crying, and if one had to laugh, he would laugh as well.

After looking around the circle to the other tools and seeing they all had closed their eyes, Walt looked at Roybe and said with a smile, "Don't look at me in that tone of your face." Roybe smiled and they both nodded their heads or shook their shoulders in agreement.

"Well we might as well follow suit," said Roybe, one of the few times he has taken the initiative to be a leader or to at least speak like one. There was silence as they all sat in a circular classroom formation, some with their hands folded in front of their chests, and others with their hands out on their laps, and Dae facing them, on the floor. The only sound to break this silence was that of the occasional thunder outside. The constant flashes of lightning produced no response from anyone.

"Indeed it was a long time ago, longer now than it seems, and in a place that only existed in our imagination, that we heard the tales handed down by our ancestors," said Dae. After Dae's opening remarks, there was a very bright flash of lightning followed by a burst of thunder. It was as if the thunder and lightning waited until Dae finished with that opening remark for it to burst. Perhaps the thunder and lighting did remain, and the noise and flash wanted everyone to hear what Dae said before it would strike again.

The thunder rolled again, but this time it was so loud if Dae had begun to speak, it would have drowned out his voice! But he paused for a moment, just long enough for the thunder to pass. Even though the thunder did not interrupt Dae's speaking, it also did not make any of the tools open up their eyes to look around to see what was going on. They all managed to keep their eyes closed as Dae spoke, and so he continued.

"As I faced north, I could see my shadow stretched out to my right, and it was much taller than I was which told me it was early evening, although I am not sure of the exact hour of the day, or the day of the week."

"In the tool shed, I saw only the top of a wooden bench on which all the tools were placed. There were no electrical tools. No tools had moving or removable parts. We were not blessed with being in the greatest of shape or with looking good. There was no constant reminder like there is today as to what the perfect tool with the perfect body should look like."

"There were so few of us back then that when our master came into the shop, depending on the time and day, we knew which one of us he wanted to use and we knew what we were going to do at that moment."

"The tools never complained about the weather outside or the working conditions inside. They were not so advanced with knowing how much pressure to apply and in what direction to go. Our master did all of that work for us. All we did was help him along the way and make life easier.

"At the end of the day, even after working for hours and hours, we never had to say, "Okay, let us sit down so we can recharge ourselves, we need energy, rest, or fuel so that we can go on. We were simple tools with simple functions and simple needs, but produced an extraordinary result."

"Outside this shed, it was a lot different than it is outside of this garage. With no rain for months and sometimes years, the vegetation had long since given way to a barren desert that now stretched out over the entire land," said Dae.

While Dae was telling this story, it appeared as if the thunder and lightning had come to an end. No one heard it anymore, and they seemed to have gotten used to the sound and the flashes of light.

Brin, at that time, was the one most familiar with cleaning away dust and dirt, so when Dae began to talk about the sand and dust, he smiled. He knew of the kind of place Dae was talking. Brin was used by the master to bush away dust not only from an ancient site but also to brush away an area that needed to be painted by the spray gun back in the garage. Being the one most familiar with the desert and its sand, Brin's ancestors were always the ones to get down and dirty with the archeologist, clearing the area around the delicate and ancient discoveries. Like everyone else sitting around and listening to Dae tell his story, Brin had no immediate comment to make of Dae's story, but he was very familiar with the area described by Dae. By his grin, it seemed that he was the only one comprehending what Dae was talking about.

Dae continued telling his tale:

"The owner of the shed where we were housed was a humble man, a man who liked uncomplicated things and had a very uncomplicated life. His name was Joseph. He shared his house along with his wife, Mary. It's believed that they were both in their thirties and at the time had no kids.

Joseph was a caring, energetic, confident man, but gentle and careful in his work. He was the kind of man everyone in the village knew they could call upon to help them with their own miscellaneous projects in and around the house. When called upon, no matter the reason, complexity or simplicity of the project, he would gladly take it on, time permitting, without asking anything in return.

In return for his good standing with the people of the community, Joseph and Mary were rewarded with what some would term, the best of luck.

It appeared at least on the outside that nothing wrong had ever happened to them. They always displayed their cheerful and upbeat side throughout the day, week, month, year and life, in general.

Mary was as gentle, if not gentler than her husband in every manner of everyday life. She was simple, yet sophisticated, in that no matter the illness or problem the townsfolk encountered, she was the one woman everyone in the village could rely on. They were comfortable enough with her to talk to or ask her for ideas and or help. Whether it was to offer advice or to prescribe the right homemade remedy to fix any ailment, they all would refer each other via word of mouth to her. Sometimes all she had to do was to talk to someone and hug them to make them feel much better in an instant. But first and foremost in her life was her dedication and loyalty to her husband, and that was never compromised.

Likewise, she was first and foremost in his book; they placed themselves second only to each other.

Like most ordinary days, Joseph, being the best known local carpenter, was wearing his traditional long white robe, with what looked like a headscarf wrapped around his head and a black rope that substituted as a belt tied around the waist. He walked into his tool shed and stood in the doorway taking in a deep breath of the crisp morning air, all the while glancing at his tools, and his woodpile in a corner on the other side of the shed.

This shed was made primarily of mud and branches. It had open windows on the sides and an entrance and an exit at opposite ends of the dwelling. It had long leaves hanging down the corridor and over the window that acted as a curtain of sorts. Their tools, animals, and personal belongings were never locked up like we were in a garage. There were no locks on anything, whether that be the house or shed.

In the foreground were two of the recently completed baby rockers he made for two different families from another village. These baby rockers or wooden cribs, had carved wooden rails on the sides, and a curved wooden headboard and footboard so the baby could be rocked from side to side until he or she fell asleep.

In those days, however, these baby rockers or cribs were known as mangers.

Only the very wealthy could afford one of these custom built mangers. They could also be purchased by going into the next significant town which had a vast open market every Saturday morning. The market operated from sunrise to sunset where the town's folks could buy, sell and trade the goods and services they had for the ones they needed. The rich could barter with something they had a lot of, for perhaps an animal or some domestic services. For the poor and budget-conscious however, they would have to rely on a friend or family; or in the case of the severely poor and isolated, they would have to rely on someone like Joseph to help them out. Joseph stood at the entrance and looked around, but before he could utter a word out loud, his wife Mary walked in behind him and tapped him gently on his shoulder and whispered, 'It is time for breakfast, dear.'

Breakfast consisted of bread and whatever meat was captured the day before, as well as hot tea, which was made from leaves and whatever grains were either grown in the backyard, or picked up at the local market, or swapped for Joseph's carpentry skills. Also, it could be what someone gave to Mary for her kindness. Whatever was served for food never got a single complaint from either Joseph or Mary.

Joseph turned toward his wife, smiled and placed his right hand on her hand over his left shoulder to at least acknowledge her. He then turned around, while still holding her hands, smiled without uttering a word, and walked with her hand-in-hand out the door.

With their eyes still closed while Dae was telling his story, they could hear that the thunder had indeed stopped. The sound of the wind outside, had also died down. There was now a new smell in the air, a scent that was not at all common to this region. They could experience all of this through the words of Dae talking his story.

Joseph was now out of the shed and no longer blocked their view of what was ahead of them. The tools were in awe of what was in their midst as they strolled down the middle of the shed. Their eyes lit up as they looked around the shed seeing what it contained. They were indeed amazed as to how different it was from the garage where they came from.

This new place had no walls for the tools to be hung on; Everything was laid out on top of a wooden bench on one side of the shed. There was no electrical outlet on the wall, no air compressor to plug the tools into or air hose to clean them off after every use, and no extension cords stretching across the floor. In a word, it was primitive.

Looking from side to side, Ed and Walt gave a friendly wave and smile now and again to everything they saw in the shed along the way. Nothing waved back or even acknowledged them, but they still waved.

The things in the shed, lying on the wooden bench, included an old sword, a large feather, as well as a tall broom, similar to Brin in design, but noticeably larger.

It had a much longer handle, the same in circumference but ten times as long at its base. It was also more than twenty times wider than Brin was.

Brin had dark brushes with a golden tip while this brush had a sort of faded yellow look to it in both its handle and brush.

Looking at the tools on the wooden bench, Walt could not help but notice that there were no electrical cords to plug. He also saw that there were no tools on the top that had a long cord attached to them. He thought to himself, "only tools such as he was, the tools of the future, came without wires and cords," so this was puzzling to him.

"Wow, look ma, no cord," said Walt sarcastically as he pointed at them.

"Yes but these guys do not need cords or outlets to do their job here," Dae responded.

"How in the world do they survive on their own without any electricity?" Walt continued as he looked around the shed and was aware that everything was new at least to him.

"That is what I will explain if you let me," Dae countered.

"Out here, in addition to no electricity for them to use, there was also no oil to keep them lubricated, and they had to rely on their owners strength to get the job done. Their owner would hold them and guide them having him do all the work using no horsepower.

The tools on the counter, the sword, broom and feather, one by one, jumped down off the table and lined up in front of the visiting tools, eyes wide open staring them in the face. Not in a threatening manner, but more of "who are you?" as they looked each other up and down and side to side to see just what they were.

The sword, bright and shiny and almost the same length as the broom, standing with his pointed edge to the floor and the handle up in the air, was the first to speak.

Raising his hands in the air wide open, he said, "Hi my name is Swordan. Let me take this moment to welcome you all to our world. I have heard from my grandparents that the tools of the future will be different in their features and design, and have a lot more power, and be able to do some amazing things, but I never thought I would see any of them in my lifetime. Tell me, where are you guys from, and what are you doing here?"

Brin, Porter, and Ed were amazed at this new old tool in their midst. This guy already knew that they were from another time and place and that they were tools of the future. A million questions ran through their minds, such as "Who was this tool?" and "How did he know we were from the future? and "How did his grandparents and great-grandparents know this?"

Even looking around and seeing what they could see in front of them did not yield any immediate answers. Instead, it only brought on more questions. They were curious as to what the answers would be, but for now, the initial shock was the fact that the sword knew of them so well.

"Where we come from, there are no tools in use like you guys today," said Brin, to Swordan, the broom, and the feather.

There was a gasp of "ahhhh" as they were surprised to hear that they were not in use anymore, at least not as tools.

"Then where are we?" asked Swordan.

"You guys are all mostly in movies, museums, and used as ceremonial pieces for the Marines, and midevil shows," Dae continued.

The broom then walked up. "Hello my name is Kati," said the broom, "and my feather friend here is Arial."

"What is a museum?" asked Kati, "and what are the Marines?"

"Well, first off, let me tell you about the museums. It is a place where artifacts, as you are now called, live on forever. It is a place where people from all walks of life come to see how things from the past were used, how they operate and function," said Dae. "And as for the Marines, they are a branch of the military, our defense department, and they use your relatives for ceremonies, etc."

"So we are not used in wars anymore? Not used on the great battlefields to charge forward at the enemy?" asked Sworden.

"No, you are not," said Dae.

"So we are not dead?" asked Kati.

"Oh no," said Dae. You live on in museums, movies, TV, and books."

"What's a movie, and what is TV?" asked Kati.

"Oh it is a long story," said Dae. "But let me assure you guys, you do live on forever. It's just that your functionality has changed and your role in life has changed as well."

"It will certainly be interesting to see where and how you guys will adjust and fit in here, though," said Swordan.

There was silence. No one thought about their role and how they would fit in here. The new tools with their electrical cords and batteries had no place plug into, and tools like Roybe had nothing to cut.

"And what about us, the feathers?" asked Arial.

"Well, you guys live on forever as well, and you are all over the place," said Dae. "You guys are everywhere now, although your functions have taken on new meaning and different forms. For starters, somewhere along the way, a liquid called ink came along, people would use your relatives to dip one end into the ink and write, but not on tablets or walls, but on something else, a new thin light product we call paper.

Paper is an item that comes from the trees. These trees are also a distant relative of yours, the pencil. We also use pens to write with," said Dae.

"You mean I have relatives?" asked Arial.

"Yes you have many," said Dae.

"The pen, who is he or she?" asked Arial.

"Well, like I said, somewhere along the way a thing called ink came about, and it was a liquid that everyone would dip your relatives into to write. Later, someone figured out a way to place it into a tube and added a little ball on the tip of the tube that blocked the hole to the tube where only a little bit of the ink could get out at a time. When this ball would roll along the surface of the paper, it would leave a trail of ink behind it. A skilled individual could use this to create words that came together to form sentences and sentences that came together to form paragraphs, and onto stories like the one I am now telling you," said Dae.

"These pens are of many races, too. There are black, yellow, blue, red, green, just about every different color you can think. Yes, your family is truly multi-cultural."

"And what about my cousin, the pencil?" asked Arial.

"Oh yes," said Dae. "Well, as I said, they are made of lead and enclosed in a tube, and most of these tubes are made of wood.

These cousins of yours work the same way as the pens do. When the pencil first came about, it stayed firmly in one piece. Nowadays, however, people are using a mechanical pencil, and some use what we call a computer, and I fear that this new tool will soon make your relatives, the pens and the pencils obsolete as well. This new tool, the machine, does everything a pen and pencil can do and then some, but that is a whole other story," said Dae.

"Are we also in museums?" asked Arial.

"Well, some of you are in museums, but they are the ones that are closest to you in this period of time, ones that are so old and rare and exotic, like the ones used to sign important documents. Those are the ones that end up there."

"Are we in museums as well?" asked Kati.

"Yes, you are used in cleaning the museum floors," said Porter sarcastically.

Kati gave Porter a stern look.

"Don't look at me in that tone of face," Porter said laughing.

"No, you are not in a museum," said Dae, "but you have changed quite a bit over the years. Some of the brooms of the future are made of, plastic, and some are mechanical, and others have electrical components. Unlike sweepers like you, these suck up the dirt and debris instead of moving it around. They are what we call motorized brooms. The operator can then take this collected dirt and dump it out somewhere in a trash container. We call these brooms of the future vacuums. There are also vacuums that can suck up water as well as dirt."

"Wow, that must be quite a sight! Very amazing!" said Kati. "I wish I could see that sometime."

Swordan, Brin, and Arial listened to all Dae had to say, and then they approached the new tools and one by one extended their hands to each of them.

"Would you like to see outside?" asked Arial.

Everyone nodded as Kati led the way to the door that led out the back.

"Oh, wow," was the most common comment coming from the new tools as they made their way outside, but all they could see before them was a vast desert as far out as the horizon. With dunes and dust clouds moving back and forth. Skeletons of dead animals that could not make it to water and or food to continue their journey littered the area here and there.

"What is this place? How can you or anyone live here? What is there to do? What is there to build?" asked Walt. "There is nothing to build and nothing to see out here."

"It was raining when we left. There was more free flowing water than we could imagine and now I am here, and it is drier than anything I have ever seen," said Walt

"Lordy, sometimes I think that the only way I can be happy is if I am around people that are miserable," said Porter. But his comment was not aimed directly at anyone.

Swordan, Kati, and Arial were a tad confused as to what Walt was talking about, or how he was behaving. Never before had they encountered anyone that would complain or was dissatisfied with what they had in front of them or with life in general. Complaining and not appreciating what they had was something new to them. "Why would anyone complain about too much free-flowing water?" they asked.

"Are you not happy with what you have?" asked Swordan, of Walt.

"How can you be happy?" Walt responded as he threw his hands in the air, looking around.

"Look at this place, just look at this place," he said.

"But we have everything out here that we need, or ever needed, or that we ever want," said Kati.

"I was so used to getting things done, so used to looking around my area and knowing exactly what I had to do. I knew exactly what I could do to make things better, and where I would be working, but now the uncertainty of this place gives me the creeps," said Walt, raising his hands a few times as he was speaking.

For the first time in their lives, Swordan, Kati, and Arial stood there with puzzled, confused look on their face. They had never experienced anything like this before today. It was a new emotion. They had heard of this thing called sadness, and they now thought that this was something that the new tools brought here, a new illness, and it was about to become contagious. They feared that this new illness, if left unchecked would infect all of the other tools and everything else for that matter in the area. They did not know how to contain it, prevent it from spreading, or treat it. They feared it was even more terrifying than the illness itself.

Walt stopped talking and was silent for a few seconds. It was an uncomfortable few seconds and even painful. Kati, Swordan, and Arial, for the first time in their lives, were feeling the emotion of sadness. Walt was disappointed. His sorrow and disappointment were bringing everyone else down. Yes, the infection of grief was spreading, and it needed to be addressed, if not contained.

LOEPANDA

This silence did not last too long however, because where the tools were standing, they could see the sand on the sloops of the dunes began to run down the sides. Their fragile peace and tranquil surroundings were now challenged.

It was as if there were birds in a tree, and someone threw something at one of the branches. All the tools did not immediately notice it, but Walt was the first to see it, and not long after that, the others did as well. There was some mumbling among the tools as to what was happening. Porter suggested that it was a minor earthquake or maybe it was preparation for a major one.

No one panicked at first, although they all knew what an earthquake was. The others could figure out what one felt like, just by seeing it on the news.

"This was too slight to be an earthquake," said Dae.

"When I left, it was raining outside, and no one wanted to go outside. Now I am outside and no one wants to be outside," said Roybe. Everyone erupted in laughter.

"This is no earthquake," said Ariel. "As I stand here on this sand, I can feel the earth beneath me, and it is not moving. Believe you me, the ground talks to me, and right now it is telling me that all the movement is confined to the surface," he continued.

As the tools looked around the desert to see if the entire place was indeed moving, it became apparent that the whole area was not moving. It was moving in front of them just a few feet. A scorpion came walking up to them and made the ground shake more and more heavily with every step. He stopped directly in front of the tools, and the shaking of the ground stopped.

"Well we can stop wondering where this shaking was coming from now," said Swordan.

The harmless brown scorpion wore nothing but a hat and a pair of sunglasses. His thin tail came up to the tools, but at first, he did not say a word.

Due to his size, everyone had to look down at him.

Swordan, Kati, and Arial were familiar with the scorpions in this area, although not this one in particular. They had seen and encountered as well as befriended one or two in this dessert before.

The other tools had only seen them on television and in the movies. Usually horror films where they sting, then kill their victims in a matter of minutes.

None of the tools was particularly worried though, because all of its victims were humans of flesh and blood, so they were trying more to figure out its purpose than its threat.

Except for Swordan, Kati, Arial, and Dae, everyone was left to wonder who this new thing is standing in front of them.

"Hi," said the scorpion, facing the tools. "My name is Loepanda."

Starting with Walt, he asked, "Where are you from? I have never seen anything like you out here before," he said.

"Are you poisonous?" asked the Scorpion, as he rolled up his thin tail with a smirk.

"No, I am not," said Walt.

"Oh, I was looking at your long pointed front and thought you were like me, only from the future or perhaps another place and time," said Loepanda, as he used his tail to scratch his head.

"So who are you? "What are you doing out here? Where are you from? and Where are you going?" asked Walt.

"Wow, one question at a time," Loepanda replied, holding one of his hands up in the air, and using the other one to remove his sunglasses.

"As I said, my name is Loepanda, and I am a reporter, and I am here to get reports on any new projects in the area."

He took out a feather and notepad from under his hat as if he were about to take notes on what they were going to discuss.

Arial liked this and smiled. He knew of this other writing instrument that Dae had just, explained to him, but he said nothing publicly.

"You mean to tell me that you are out here looking for new projects? By that I mean, as far as the eye can see, do you think that there are new projects out here to report on?" said Walt.

"Well, you never know," said Loepanda. "It seems as though every time I go to a new town or area, I always encounter something new or different along the way, like the first time I came to a place like this. I have never been here before though, and I found you guys, and you are all new to me, so this will give me something new to write home about.

"Are we the first and the only new thing you have had to write home about?" asked Walt.

"Well, actually, yes, you guys are the first new and exciting things I have had to write home about," Loepanda replied.

"Oh, but I would say though, the one thing you guys have to look out for out here is vultures. They fly around looking for strange things that are not moving, so they can swing down and eat them dry," Loepanda told the tools.

"If I had not run into you guys and I came across one of them, I would have to write about them again this time around."

Again, except Dae, Swordan, Kati, and Arial, no one knew what a vulture was, or had any idea what it might look like since Loepanda did not describe it in detail except to say it can fly. All they knew was that it was to be avoided and perhaps it would come in silently from above.

"Have you guys seen the vultures?" asked Porter of Swordan and Kati.

After looking at each other and then back to Porter, they nodded their heads to respond, "yes." "Well, we have seen a vulture before, but I am not sure which one of the vultures he is referring to."

"We have not seen them out here, but we have heard terrible stories about them," said Swordan.

"So to avoid being captured by these vultures, you have to kick up sand and keep moving. Do not stand around looking like you are dead, so walk with me," said Loepanda, as he turned around and began to walk ahead of the tools in a direction farther away from the shed. No one hesitated to follow him, and no one questioned him and his leadership, either including Dae.

Loepanda walked and talked with them into the heart of the desert, and as he did this, he would stick the tip of the feather in his mouth and then place it on the notepad he had which was made of pieces of leaves from a maple tree.

He had one leaf on top of the other, and he would take notes, although he did not relay to them what he was writing down. As he was walking and talking to them, it was apparent the things he would talk about were general but provided all the answers to the questions they would have. These notes included, where they came from, what they did, and what they thought about the place. As the day went on, it was slowly turning into evening.

To the tools, it did not appear as though they had walked very far, or that they talked about anything much either, but it occurred to them that the day had somehow flown by them in a matter of minutes. The day seemed to go by a lot faster out here than it did back home. No one noticed the time, whether they were enjoying themselves too much, or they had too many questions for which there were too few answers, or as Dae put it, "time flies when you encounter new circumstances."

So they must have been having fun or were preoccupied with their new surroundings.

They came to a cool spot under a dune that was high enough in the air that it provided some shade. They walked away from the sunset following Loepanda in his steps and they stopped walking when he stopped.

"At night it will get painfully cold out here," said Loepanda.

"We should gather up some brush to make a fire then," said Walt.

"And what will we use to light this fire?" asked Ed.

"That's the easy part," said Swordan.

"You have me, and you have Roybe here. We will bump against each other, and you will see sparks fly," he said as he grabbed Roybe around the wrist and said, "Come on now, hit me with all you got."

"Watch this," said Swordan, as he raised himself in the air and came down hard, hitting Roybe on the side of his blade. Roybe did not budge or appear to feel any pain with the striking of Swordan against him.

Sure enough, sparks started to fly, and before long it there were so many sparks in the air from Swordan striking Roybe so many times, and so rapidly, it looked like a fourth of July fireworks show. The other tools and Loepanda were very impressed. They quickly ran off to help gather up some dried-up bones from all the skeletons, as well as some dried brush to help make the fire. This took a matter of a few minutes and they managed to gather enough firewood to maintain a fire that they hoped would keep each other warmed up all night and brought it back to the base camp.

"We need to dig a hole," said Dae "And not just any hole, but a big hole to put all the bones and brush into it and keep it stable so we can have a good fire."

"I'll help with the hole," said Swordan, as he and Dae began to dig their hole, while the others watched from the sides.

The hole dug was about four feet across and no more than one foot deep.

It was sufficient for the bones and brush, yet it allowed them to dig it and be finished quite quickly.

Up to this point, with the day just coming to a close, there had been no vultures.

"Perhaps it is just an urban legend, these stories about the vultures. Maybe that is just something people say to frighten children. That's my church, but we will just have to wait and see," said Porter.

'That's your church?" said Loepanda, "What does that mean?"

"It means, that's my belief," replied Porter.

No one said a word. A few minutes turned into more than an hour until the silence was felt throughout the area. It seemed no one was going to go into detail and try to explain Porter's slang to Loepanda and the others.

No one said anything for so long that slowly but surely everyone just fell asleep.

The next day, after spending the night bundled up together in a pile, everyone awoke somewhat stiff from not moving around much the night before.

Sleeping on the ground was a new thing. Too many of them were used to hanging on a wall hook and being suspended in the air. There was plenty of space and time for all to stretch out. For the most part, it felt as though they had worked all night and they were very tired. Their muscles were aching.

No sooner had they gotten up, then here came Walt again, complaining about how stiff his back was, and how tired he felt. Although everyone else was tired and stiff, no one at first was really complaining about it. His complaints were numerous, but now they were not all from Walt. This time he got some help from Porter as well.

Arial, Kati, and Swordan had nothing to complain about, nor did Dae. They simply got up and were refreshed and ready to begin their day as if nothing had happened.

Seeing that they were not getting any sympathy from the others, all of the complainings began to dwindle and soon stopped.

The sun was now waking up, and even though it was early in the morning, they could tell it was going to be a very hot day ahead of them.

Noticeably absent from the sounds the tools were used to hearing in the morning, was the sound of roosters letting everyone know morning was ringing their doorbell. The heat from the sun was enough to wake everyone up.

There weren't any questions about breakfast or anything to eat or getting refueled or recharged in any way. There weren't even any questions about where they would acquire food or as to where they would have to hunt for food or any of those sorts of thing from Loepanda.

Everyone just wanted to know what the plans were for the day ahead. Dae hinted to Loepanda for ideas as to what was the plan for the day ahead, but he did it in such a clever way, it was not noticed by anyone. Since Loepanda had led them out to this point, all they knew was that Loepanda had warned them about vultures, but looking around there was no sign of the so-called vultures. The only thing they could see ahead of them was sand, sand, and more sand, with bones and an occasional dried-up bush rolling past them here and there.

The old tools were eager to demonstrate to the new tools their home life, their way of life, the things they could do, the things they had done, and the things they would like to do, the things that did not require electricity.

Seeing something they did not get to see in their old home, every day like the sunrise, was nice. Now and then, perhaps, they would see it if they were outside working very early on a project, but definitely not every day.

Now that they had seen something from the old tools' home life surroundings, they would like to show them something as well. Back in the newer tools place, their home was the garage of a house that sat near the middle of the city, and seeing the sunrise over the horizon is not something they were used to. Their view was blocked by skyscrapers.

Here the sun would rise above the sand dunes, and it was spectacular.

It was now clear they were going to continue on a path that was yet to be determined, led by Loepanda, followed by Brin, who quickly ran out in front to clear a path for the others. Dae began to walk over to the fire hole and was piling back the sand that he helped to dig last night for a fire. Dae was not alone however, in covering this hole up. Roybe used his blade to assist by pushing the sand back over the hole, as did Swordan. The three of them worked together until the hole was completely covered back up.

Stan, and Walt just followed along not sure what their use was and what, if anything, they could do.

After several minutes that seemed like hours of walking they stopped for a while to catch their breath, stopping only long enough to notice a shadow from overhead that passed them on the ground. Brin, still walking ahead of all the other tools, came to a stop.

"What was that?" asked Walt.

"I wonder, too," said Porter.

"That, my friend was a vulture," said Swordan. "If he comes around again, I am going to flip and cut him down." Swordan seemed unmoved by the vulture. Porter was somewhat shaken by the mysterious creature and, not knowing what to expect from the vulture and not wanting to appear as if he was scared of it, he hid his fears well. They looked around, trying to see what it was going to do next, and where it would come in from next. All of a sudden, they heard a loud scream, a scream that led Loepanda to bury his head in the sand and say, "This is who I warned you guys about!"

Loepanda soon enough buried most of its body into the sand, while all the other tools were exposed. It seemed as though Swordan and Dae were the only two not even showing any signs of concern.

Suddenly, like the bolts of lightning that struck when the tools were back in their home, all of that was about to end. The scenery was too perfect and calm when appearing out of what seemed to be nowhere, was the vulture for everyone to see close up. Panic struck the area! Almost everyone (except Swordan and Dae) wanted to do like Loepanda had done and bury their bodies in the sand. But at the same time, they all knew that was not the best thing to do in this particular situation. It was not realistic.

"Come on, guys, there is no way on earth we can let this thing scare us, we outnumber him," said Swordan.

"Fear is a feeling just like being cold or hot. Remember, last night we felt cold, and to overcome it, we lit a fire to counter it. When you get hot, you seek shelter in a shaded, cool place and drink cool liquid. Well, fear is the same thing. When you get scared, you seek corrective action and stand up against what you are scared of. To avoid the vulture and not be his next meal, you have to keep moving. Standing still tells it that you are dead, and he will come down and have you for his next meal," Swordan continued.

Swordan's words reminded the tools of Dae. They were words the tools had heard in the past as coming only from Dae.

"Around here, you move, get out of the way, or be consumed," Loepanda tells the tools.

Except for Swordan and Dae, the tools were showing signs of being scared on the outside. They had a worried look on their faces and moved closer to each other for comfort with the belief that there is safety in numbers.

No one was running off anywhere or trying to hide as Loepanda did at first. It was as if it would not be cool for a macho tool to do so. Come to think of it, with Loepanda the only one buried in the sand, the questions that would have perhaps challenged them more were, "What were they going to hide under or behind? and "Where, out here, were any of the tools going to run off to?"

"Folks, folks, look at us, we are not made of flesh and blood. There is no way for him to eat us, so we do not have to be afraid of him. You noticed all the scattered bones you passed when you were walking over here. Well, they are all of the things that have flesh and blood. The vultures are meat eaters, not metal magnets, so we have nothing to be afraid of. The only thing fear does is make us weak," said Swordan. All those stories we have heard in the past of the vultures coming down and scooping up any and everything in its path, those stories are called urban legends. They only apply to the flesh and bone creatures that move about down here, therefore, we are not on his menu. He is merely checking us out. I tell you what, the next time he comes around, I want us all to stand still and not move or run for cover and see what happens," Swordan continued.

With it being what they thought was around high noon the tools looked up, all they could see bearing back down on them was the sweltering sun, relentless in its heat. This heat did not bother the tools. They were used to generating a lot of heat in whatever projects they were involved in. The bright sun was blocking their view of the vulture. Even though it was continually flying around, going far out into the horizon and coming back, it was slightly outside the path of the sun and therefore provided no shadow for the tools to see exactly where he was over their heads.

The vulture came around again, but this time he came close to the ground, just slightly above the heads of the tools. A few of the devices, Porter, Roybe, and Ed, ducked their heads, not that they were scared, but as if the vulture was about to grab one of them. The tools feared being picked up and taken far out into the desert, then dropped off when it finds out they're not food. From there, the tools would have to find their way back by themselves. All the other tools stood still.

Swordan did as he said: a backflip and landed on his head with his sharp-pointed side up in the air for the vulture to see. The vulture flew over once more and appeared as if it was ready to circle again. On this pass, however, Brin ran over to join Swordan and decided to stand up to it as well.

"Let's show this thing that we are not afraid of it," said Brin.

As the vulture got closer to the tools and then directly over their heads, Brin kicked up some dust into its eyes. By rapidly brushing the sand up in the air it created a dust cloud for the vulture. Walt and Roybe, although used to dust from cutting and drilling wood back home, started to cough from all the dust being kicked up.

Swordan began waving back and forth as if he were cutting something in the air. The vulture did not like this and, decided that he had no meal here. He encountered resistance, something he could not get used to. Instead of swooping down over the tools like he would have done, he just rose up and flew higher.

The vulture realized two things: not only did he not have any food here, but he also had living things that were not afraid of him, and they were going to fight back should he land near them. They were at least willing to put up some resistance by fighting back. But like a bully in the schoolyard, vultures love having defenseless opponents. The vulture was not used to things fighting back. Targets were usually helpless and only just lay there and let him have his way.

"See, see what I told you?" said Swordan. "Nobody likes a bully. We come together and stand up to him, so he realized that he was outnumbered, outgunned, and he simply cannot win this fight, so he got out of here and went on his way."

Everyone got up and started dusting themselves off. The tools all looked at Dae who was standing on top of the ground near where Loepanda buried its body for cover. They admired him for not moving or appearing to be scared of the vulture as it flew over.

"Lord, why did you not duck and run for cover out of the way as the others did?" asked Porter, approaching Dae.

"If we ran away from the things that fear us the most, we would be running forever.

For someone who runs and hides in the face of danger will never have the courage and inclination to understand the true meaning of being free," Dae responded.

Dae would continue as he has always done before. He is never satisfied with just uttering one sentence or phrase regarding a situation. He has to say several corresponding quotes to get his point across; he feels that rephrasing himself works better for the tools' comprehension, so he continued to speak.

"He who hides from danger is afraid of himself. Unless we stand up and face what frightens us, we will always and forever be on the run from our fears. Fear is the darkness that runs until the light of courage catches up to it."

Stan and Walt turned to Dae and asked him what he thinks of the tools' purpose in this strange new world; not everyone uses a hammer and a drill every day.

Perhaps they do so now and again, but in this world, where as far as the eye can see it is just sand and emptiness. There was not only a reason to question their existence, but also anyone's reason for wanting to live out here.

Porter stared around the desert and thought to himself that he did not see any use for his talents either.

"There is no wood or nail to put anything together. In fact, there weren't even any metals," said Porter.

Stan, now sounding a little depressed after listening to Porter, raised his hand in the air and told everyone to listen to him for a second and they did. "You know, in my home, I felt that you and I could do things. You and I together could build things. I could put things together, but out here, there is nothing for me to build or put together, practically nothing for me to do. I, too, feel useless," he said as he bowed his head as if to sob.

Dae, could not comprehend why everyone seemed to be feeling so depressed. Then he thought that after what they had just gone through with the vulture, (which was enough to spook them), that that was why they sounded so depressed. Also, they were in a new place, experiencing new things and meeting new people. That could also cause depression.

Dae just knew it was the fear of the unknown, the fear of not knowing where they were heading, the fear of the unpredictable, the lack of control and the feeling of weakness the tools had. Not knowing what was to come, or what was to be the outcome, what they would encounter next, and how they would handle it, etc., all contributed to the depression.

As they all stood around in the increasingly hot sun, Dae patted Stan on his shoulder to comfort him and assured him he was not out of place or alone, and everything will be all right.

"I am confident you will find a meaningful use one day. It does not have to be out here, it does not have to be today, but life always finds a way and use for everything and everyone," said Dae. "Sometimes for you to determine what you need to do, you simply have to take a look around you and see what needs to be done," Dae continued.

"You know, whenever I am feeling sad, I think of the first thing I ever built by myself. I think about how difficult it was to build it, and the uncertainty that I had as to how it would turn out. I was not sure of all I had to do to get it done correctly, and if it would turn out the way I envisioned it. Once I got started, I could not stop. Once I got over the first obstacle, it was on to the next, and then the next. Soon I was moving right along as if I knew what I was doing, and once it was completed, it was like riding a bike. Once you get the hang of it, it becomes second nature. Then you go about your life building all the other things you want to build just like that, and it too becomes second nature. Before you know it, you are happy, without even trying and that is what leads to success. The path to life, like being happy is also a feeling like that of being afraid. Being happy is a state of mind. To be truly happy, you have to show others that you are happy, and help others to become happy as well. Yes, happiness, like bad attitudes and sadness is also contagious."

Stan smiled at Dae. He felt the feeling he longed for when he missed the spot when Sam was using him to drive the nail into the wall earlier, or the feeling you get if someone pats you on the back and praises you for a job well done. Whatever the reason, he seemed much happier now.

PEBBLE

A rock, lying in the foreground that could not help but overhear Stan and Dae speaking woke up and said, "hi."

He was oval about six inches long and weighed about two and a half pounds, smooth on the underneath and choppy on the top. His underneath was noticeably a lighter color than his head. You can see his top was where he exposed to the sun for a considerable length of time.

Until this rock moved, no one had even noticed he was there. It was as if he blended into the landscape somehow. He was hidden because he was camouflaged with the sand, the sand that was now removed by the light wind. He turned to Stan in particular and smiled because he could not help overhearing him for he had been listening to Dae as well, and he wanted to cheer Stan up some more.

He approached Stan with a gleaming look on his face. Stan did not back away from him as the other tools looked on.

"I understand what you were going through and I understand what you were feeling. You have nothing to be afraid of, or be depressed about," the rock said to Stan.

Walt looked at the rock and said, "As I live and breathe, I could not figure out what I could do in this place, but now, looking at you, I do not feel as bad now." Everyone laughed.

The rock appeared to be unmoved by Walt's comment. "Look at me. In your world, I am sure your people would have no use for me either, but out here these people have plenty of uses for me," the rock said, with his arms wide open.

"By the way, my name is Pebble, that's, P-E-B-B-L-E," said the rock.

"And what is your name?" asked Pebble.

"Stan," he replied.

"Is it short for something?" asked Pebble, scratching his head. "I'll bet you have never heard of me or anyone like me have you?" asked Pebble.

"No, honestly I have to say I have not. I have seen rocks before, from all walks of life, but you are the first of your kind I have ever seen," Stan replied. "I have never seen one come up and talk to me, claiming that they understood what I was going through or even offering to help, I never met a rock that had feelings."

Pebble walked up a little closer and stood directly in front of Stan. He reached out and patted Stan on his shoulder, as Dae had, and said, "Son, if you were to look beyond your current form, you would discover that you and I are not just alike, but we share a common ancestry."

Stan was now more confused than he had ever been. Here was someone he had never met in his life or ever heard of, who was telling him that they shared a common ancestry. Stan was not one to try to trace his family tree, so this guy had no meaning to him.

Stan paused for a moment and stared at Pebble with his head tilted to one side, then looked again and tilted his head to the other side. Bringing his head now to the upright position, he placed his hand on his chin and said, "You know, I do not see any resemblance. I am a hammer, I drive nails into wood, and I remove nails from wood, and I have also worked with some archeologist. You, on the other hand, are a rock. They use you to build roads and wells, etc. There is no connection between the two of us."

"You should not be depressed to be out here, or feel useless. You should instead be proud because of who you are and where you came from." Pebble went on to say.

"Well, how many nails have you pulled out, how many nails have you driven into the ground or how many houses have you built, how many roofs and windows have you secured, and how many archeologists have you worked with?" Stan asked Pebble abruptly.

Pebble placed his hands on his chin, stroked his chin for a moment, looked down on the ground and then back up at Stan for a moment and then asked, "What's a nail?"

"See, you don't even know what a nail is, so how can we be related. We have nothing in common," said Stan.

"Open your eyes and look beyond what you see in front of you. You will be amazed," said Pebble.

"You know, I think that you are more related to Dae than you are to me. You and he talk in the same tongue," said Stan.

Although Pebble had said a lot, he had not said anything that made Stan conclude that the two were related. In fact, none of the tools could see the resemblance or connection between the two of them either. He had yet to explain the relationship between him and Stan in a way that they could understand.

"Your ancestors like him have done quite a bit for society, said Stan."

"I am being replaced in the new world by this," said Stan, as he pointed to Porter, the one that was now being used to drive nails into wood, a job he used to have.

"When we left, it was raining, and it had been doing so for hours due to a slow-moving storm we call a hurricane, a storm we knew was coming so we all were prepared for it," said Stan. "It was a storm in which all the doors and windows had to be boarded up around the house, a job I did not take part in. Porter had all the glory," Stan continued.

"Before he came along, whenever there was a storm like this, I would be the one used to board up the windows and doors to prevent the wind from blowing things into the house or structure and doing any damage to the interior. Whenever a storm was planning on coming through, I was the one called upon to prepare for it. I took center stage," said Stan.

"You, my distant relative, have not seen rain from an expected storm like your ancestors and I have seen rain," said Pebble.

"I am sure that the rain will come to an end eventually, perhaps a few minutes or a few hours from now, but it will end."

"Let me assure you, the rain that you are talking about now is nothing compared to the rain we have had out here," Pebble went on to say.

"You mean to tell me that this place had rain once upon a time?" asked Porter, pointing around the desert.

Stan looked puzzled as he asked Pebble to please explain. Porter turned to Pebble as well and said, "Yes, please do explain, because I think Stan is not alone in his confusion. I sure would like to know more about this rain you are talking about."

"Well, if it rained here at one point, there has got be some vegetation, a sign, perhaps a tree, a dried-up lake or pond, or different colors in the sand and rock formations. Such would distinguish what was once moist and what was not, just something as to what was here before all this sand arrived," said Stan.

"Yes, yes, I also would like to know what you are talking about," said Ed.

A mumble sounded throughout the crowd as everyone agreed that they would like to know as well.

"That I will explain," said Pebble, with one finger in the air and nodding his head.

"You see all the land around you," he said as he pointed in a circular motion.

"Well, once upon a time this was fertile land, and it contained a big village, well, big by our standard, and lots of not just people, but also plants and animal life. It was busy with excitement."

Pebble then pointed to the shed in the distance that the tools came out of and said, "An old man lived in a shed just like this one but a long time before this current guy. He was a humble man, and he did not live alone. People often said he would talk to himself, others said he heard voices that told him to do things. He would often act upon the words that these voices spoke only to him, telling him what to do.

"The old man had one of, if not the most unusual houses in the area. All of the other houses in the village were built flat to the ground, but he built high above the ground on rocks that were large enough to elevate the house about three feet off the ground."

"Where are those rocks now," asked Ed. "Looking at this shed now, I can see that it is sitting flat down on the ground. Did they sink into the ground or something?" asked Ed.

"Well, let me finish the story, and I will explain that, and you will get a better understanding as to what happened here, a long, long time ago," said Pebble.

"Oh, okay, please continue then," said Ed.

"His house also was the first to be built with openings on the sides for air to come into and pass through the house. All of the other houses had just one opening into and out of the house. He called these side openings vents so named because it was where he went to cool off whenever he was getting hot from working on a project, or where he went whenever he felt frustrated and wanted to blow off some steam. He would go there to inhale and exhale for a bit and cool down. His house also had the unusual design of having an entrance in the front and the back. Unprecedented back then, but for someone whom everyone thought was a crazy man, he thought it was quite normal."

"Outside of his house, hanging on the sides all around, was where he kept many of his plants. On some nights, and especially during the winter when it got unbearably cold, he would bring these plants into the house. He would care for these plants as if they were human as if they were an extended part of his family, and they deserved the same love and attention as did everyone else."

"He also allowed his animals, and especially his two dogs, to enter and exit the house as often as they liked. Everyone else kept their dogs and other animals outside in their yard."

"The old man had this crazy thought claiming that his animals were creatures that were similar to that of humans, and just like humans, they were to be fed, bathed and housed so that they were protected from the elements of bad weather and the occasional abuse of strangers. It was also not unusual for him to have some of the animals inside the house for breakfast lunch and dinner, sharing a meal with the rest of his family, even eating the same food. He claimed that the voices told him to do this, and so he did."

"It had become the norm for the townsfolk to see him do the things he did, the things he claimed the voices told him to do, even though the things he did were different from everyone else, and it made him appear abnormal.

"Soon the things he did didn't seem so strange any more, even when he did something new. Everyone had come to accept him and the things he did as just part of what made him unique. It was just the way he was, so they eventually came to accepted him and left him alone."

"One day just like any other ordinary day, he had a thought. Everyone knew the thoughts he had were not so much crazy but just different. But this one was really "way out there" according to the villagers."

"He said the voice came in the form of a weatherman. This weatherman told him that he was to prepare for a storm unlike any that has ever hit the area. He also said that the voice told him that to prepare for this once-in-a-lifetime storm he had to do things and build things unlike he had ever done before, or anyone had ever seen or built. He said the voice gave him a comprehensive list of things that needed to be done. It was a list that was so enormous and detailed, that it took several tablets to get it all written down."

"Although to him, it did not appear to be an unusual command, this time it was somewhat different in the sheer scope of the project. The voice said that he had to do this because all of the animals and plant life out here depended on him to make it through this storm of a lifetime.

He also claimed that the voice said that no one else in the area could care for the plant life and animals like he could, so the sole responsibility for their care and well-being rested with him and to a lesser extent, his family.

No one in the area had ever heard of such a storm before or seen that much rain. It usually would rain for about an hour or two, but then the sun would come out again, and the plants and animals would have enough water to feed on for quite some time. When it did not rain the rivers and lakes provided all the water that everyone would need for a long time around the area." "Even during the so-called rainy season, when it did rain every day, it would rain for the most part about two hours nonstop, then there would be a break. After an hour or so, it would start up again. This would repeat throughout the entire rainy season, a season that usually lasted for about four months.

Most of the rain, when it did fall, you could look at it, and you can see it was coming from one direction, from an angle, like falling from the east and pointing west. In this incident, according to the old man, the rain would be coming from straight up, and beating down hard on them, relentless and straight down.

He said the voice told him that, this project was to be functional and very detailed. It was as if the voice told him he had to talk to all the animals at once. He would have to gather them in one particular place, for a convention of sorts, and they all had to fit under the same roof.

"The size of this project would appear to be overwhelming for this man, but he was indeed up for the challenge, and it would take some time to accomplish. After all, the voices told him how to build his house, and how to care for his animals and plants, but this time the voice went above and beyond anything that had come before, he thought."

"He said the voice also said to him that once it started to rain the water level would rise so fast that it would cover the entire land as far as the eye could see, and all in its path would perish in a watery grave. The mere thought of such destruction motivated and frightened him a little, but he was not one to back down from a challenge, or even ignore or disobey the voice. After all, this was the same voice that told him how to build his house and care for his plants and animals, that became the envy of the townspeople. It was the same voice that told him when to bring the plants inside when it would be too cold outside for them. The other townspeople never brought their plants inside for any reason, and when it got too cold, their plants and animals would often die."

"Well, just wait a minute here," said Stan. "Wouldn't the plants and some of the animals survive in that much water? I mean, after all, plants and animals do need water to feed and live off of, and I know of a lot of plants and animal life that have survived to this day, living at the bottom of the ocean and rivers and they have been doing so forever," said Stan.

"Good point Stan," said Pebble, "but let me tell you, some water is a good thing, but too much water, or too much of anything for that matter, is never a good thing."

The tools all recalled their weatherman stating that with the rain from the hurricane, the water level would trap some people in their homes, kill off a lot of the vegetation and destroy some homes. The vehicles that were not prepared to handle all that wind and water from the rain getting into their engines would be inoperable for a long time after the storm, and some might stop working altogether.

The tools thought that this kind of destruction, like the ones caused by the hurricanes, only happened to people that did not prepare themselves for these storms. Those that were prepared usually got away with minor scratches and no long-term regrets.

The severe weather they used to get with the hurricane would last for several hours at the most, but its aftermath would last for days, weeks or even months to come. Also though the initial storm would take less than one day to pass, usually life would go on, the way it was before.

"Let me continue," said Pebble. "The old man had a few animals on his farmland. After all, he was a good shepherd and caring for the animals he felt was his obligation. With his unique way of communicating with the animals, it was as though he spoke their language. While he would speak to the animals as if they were human, his wife, taking care of the plants, would do the same for the plants. In some cases, she would pat them and kiss them gently on the top, as if they were small children whom she had to nourish frequently."

"They could talk to them, give them commands and praise and they seemed to respond favorably every time. No one else in the town had that kind of effect on their plants and animals."

"While he and his wife would talk to the animals and plants, respectively, folks passing by would look at them and think 'how strange.' They would often carry on full-fledged conversations with the plants and animals in their care, even laughing while caressing them lightly," said Pebble.

"That is such a huge responsibility for someone who appears to be so unstable," said Stan.

"Indeed it was," said Pebble. "It was a responsibility that only this man, this good shepherd, was crazy enough to undertake."

"Sometimes the difference between being crazy and being brilliant is having the foresight and the courage to do the things that everyone else says he cannot do," said Dae.

"There are different degrees of craziness. People do crazy things and get themselves in trouble, and then there are those that do crazy things just because they are in love, others do crazy things and invent or discover amazing things, and yes, those who do crazy things get somewhere in life," said Dae.

"It is not entirely clear how long it took the old man to gather all of his information, and map out the diagrams for the project, or how much his sons and wife assisted him. One thing was for certain, they all contributed to getting his job done." Said Pebble.

"One day, after gathering all the instructions he needed for the project, the man went out searching for the biggest trees he could find and began to cut them down. He searched for all the tallest trees in the area. People did not own the trees he cut down. Back in those days, the trees and all the land were shared by everyone in the area."

"My great-grandfather was one of those who worked for so long and hard to help him to cut down these trees. My great-grandfather was a proud rock. He had a sharp, pointed head which could be used for cutting pretty much all the wood in the area.

The old man had my grandfather strapped onto the end of a piece of wood. Today you would call this tool an ax. He took my greatgrandfather in his right hand and struck at those trees for hours and hours and days and days, cutting down the tallest ones, the strongest ones, the fattest ones. He needed them all for this project," said Pebble.

"Wait one minute here. I have heard this story from my ancestors too," said Brin. "My ancestors said the old man used leaves from a palm tree and tied the sharp-edged rocks to a piece of wood and used it to cut down, carve, and shape the trees," said Brin.

"When he took my great-grandfather away from us, it was a sad day for all of us. We did not know what to expect or what to think. All we knew was that our great-grandfather was being taken away by this madman, but our great grandfather seemed to want to work with him. My great- grandfather knew he was working on a masterpiece project that could withstand the test of time."

"Sometime my great-grandfather would work for twelve to fifteen hours a day, taking only mini-breaks here and there, long enough to cool down before getting right back into it, and he would never complain."

"My great-grandfather would tell us these stories, at the end of the day at dinner when he was finished cutting down the trees. 'If I had to go and do it all over again, I would gladly volunteer to do it again, knowing what the result was,'" he said.

"The old man would then use my cousins, some of the other smaller rocks, and carve off these trees by scaling off the rough edges and cutting them into several pieces of wood in various shapes and sizes. Once he had the wood carved to his liking or specifications, he would also use some of the larger rocks to pound the wood into the curved slots where they interlocked into each other to form a tight, waterproof seal. He then laid the wood out side by side, and he used small sharp pieces of skinny pointed rocks to interlock the pieces of wood to each other, so many of my family were used to construct this project. In fact, one of the few times we all got to see most of our relatives was when we all worked on this project together," Pebble continued.

"Today, we call these skinny pointed pieces of rocks, nails," said Porter.

"Then there were the large rocks, those over five feet tall and over three feet across, and they weighed more than ten men combined. They would use these as anchors, and there were more than twelve of them," said Pebble.

He got help with the much larger rocks and larger pieces of wood, apparently, from his sons and their wives, whenever he had to lift the real heavy ones and put them into place. He created this carrier, and it was definitely unlike anything that had built before it."

"After many years of cutting these trees and carving them into the kind of wood he wanted, this massive carrier was finally completed."

"In those days, no one aged the way we do today. People tended to live on for hundreds of years, they seldom showed sign of aging or weakness, and people gave birth to kids when they were more than two or three hundred years old.

Some will argue that it took the old man almost one hundred years to build this project."

"It was oversized and somewhat oval with a substantially open center. It had a drop-down backdoor that could be lowered and raised to load and unload as well as to seal the back end. The top of it was in the shape of a house, and the ends hung over the sides to allow for the rainwater to run off the sides when the rain came.

This project also employed some new and unique architectural engineering. Never before had anything been built this big.

People built small boats to go fishing and traveling, but these little boats were built to handle one to four people at the most, and no animals."

"Next it was onto gathering the inventory for this massive carrier. He searched long and hard for what seemed like forever collecting a male and a female of each creature.

Some creatures he did not have in his inventory. He would then travel to the other towns and villages to gather them from the other towns' folks inventory through trade.

Since the other towns' folks from far away did not know him or had not heard of his craziness, they were more willing to help him than the people in his area. All of that traveling and negotiating also contributed to his taking so long to complete the project."

"He would also swap some of his carpentry services and good old-fashioned know-how for these animals as well. He took steps to ensure that he was adequately housing them on and around his land while he waited for them to board this large carrier, and according to the instruction of the voice he heard.

He collected enough food for the entire length of time he was to be on this vessel. This also included food that was to grow on board the ship that they could and will consume when the need arose. Included in this was plant life he would need for food and some 'pure' animals to use not just as food but for sacrifice. The other animals were for reproduction when the rain stopped."

"He went out of his way to find baby animals, because they were small and, being that he had to fit so many of them into this carrier, space was a premium."

"The day finally came, and he had now collected not only the plant and birds he needed but also two of each creature, one male, and one female. The lowered back had some of my other relatives along the walk, which were used as grips on the steps of the ramp for him and his family to walk and guide the animals.

"People would pass by and sometimes gathered from far away to watch this spectacle in progress. There was enough room to accommodate everyone in the town as well as the animals, but the people were not willing to be led into this carrier with animals. The townsfolk always thought it was odd to have their animals in their houses with them, let alone in a carrier that everyone thought was so far away from not only the ocean but also the nearest river."

"In modern society, I'm sure the city or town council would never approve a permit to build something of this magnitude, even in the middle of nowhere. They would have him committed, to say the least," said Porter.

"Entire generations of kids were born and grew up to full adulthood while this project took shape. They would often wonder when it would ever be completed, and when will this rain they have heard about since birth ever come? The old man became a source of folklore and bedtime storytelling. Kids, while growing up, would say things like, 'You are as crazy as Old Man Rain,' and 'that's something only Old Man Rain would say or do.'"

"The day finally arrived when the project was complete, and it was just about time to load everything and everyone onto the carrier. The first thing on the carrier was the twelve anchors. These were the largest of my family members. They were about 100 man-weights per rock. Back then, everything was measured and weighed in what was called man weight and man length. To measure the weight of an item, one could say it is one leg and an arm heavy, one man heavy, or several men heavy and so forth. As for length, we said it is an arm-length, a foot-long or, half-an-arm long or six-man-feet-long, etc. Since all the men were about the same weight and height, this became the standard system of measurement."

They were placed along the side of the carrier, for balance as well as stability, in holding the vessel in place once the vessel needed to be kept in one place.

He loaded these by placing smaller rocks on the ground, smaller stones that were round, this created a track to push the massive stones onto while he and his sons would push them onto the spot where he needed them to go. These small round rocks were placed on the floor and the more massive rocks were rolled up onto them. Each time we rolled the more massive anchor rocks, we would then go and pull them into place.

"Then it was all the plants followed by the birds and the flying creatures.

Onlookers would pass and gaze at this site and wonder how long this part of the operation was going to take place as well. It became the local tourist attraction. People passing by would also make comments and jokes while they laughed and pointed at the whole scene. Despite all the jokes and sometimes mean comments, the old man, and his family carried on, unmoved by all the other people that thought they were crazy.

After all the plants and birds were loaded onto the carrier, it was now time for the animals.

The animals walked onto the ramp, one male, and one female, side by side, until all were on the large wooden carrier, as it was called."

"At the end of the march, when all the animals were on the wooden carrier, the man and his wife and family, which included his three sons and their wives, were the last ones to go onto the carrier.

"Before the old man walked onto the carrier with his family at the end, he had a checklist and walked with his family throughout the carrier and around it to check and make sure he had everything he needed for the journey. This checklist did not take a few minutes to complete. It took the better part of a day to get it done right.

"As the old man and his wife and kids loaded themselves onto the wooden carrier, they waved farewell to everyone around them with a smile. The old man did remind the townspeople that if anyone else wanted to get onto the carrier, now was the time to do so."

"It was another hot, cloudless day when all this took place. It made the townspeople scratch their heads and wonder even more. In today's world, someone would have called the child and animal protective services to put an end to this," said Porter.

"The carrier was built to accommodate just his family and the animals and plant life that it was carrying. It was the voice that told him how large to build this, knowing how many people would want to go into it, so it was just the right size for its occupants. As the old man and his family waved, they also smiled at the crowd below, but it was a sad smile. It was a smile that said, yes, they knew that they were leaving, and they were happy to go, but it also said that the family was sad that all these people they had come to know over the years, they would not see any longer."

"It was also sad that everybody did not believe the old man and they had to suffer for all the wrong things they did, suffering for the negligence in caring for their plants and animals.

The smile on his family's face said that they knew that they were going to a new and improved place, perhaps a place that would make them so much happier than they were here."

"As the old man stood on the deck looking over the crowd, he asked them one last time if anyone wanted to come and join them before the door was sealed forever.

The townsfolk all laughed out loud and pointed their fingers at him and his family, laughing at them and calling them crazy."

Some of the chants coming from the crowd included, 'You are all fools.'

"How can you be led into this madness by this madman?"

"How long do you expect to be on this thing before you get bored and come down with a case of cabin fever? Which animal would you be eating first for food?" And the list went on.

"All of those comments were dismissed, as no one on the carrier responded to any of the chants that were coming from the crowd. The family just smiled and waved," said Pebble.

"So, did it start to rain right after everyone entered the carrier?" asked Stan.

"No, it did not," said Pebble. "In fact, for a few days after everyone was on it and the doors close, the townspeople were still joking as they passed by about the massive wooden carrier, in the middle of nowhere and far away from the nearest body of water. And how did this madman manage to convince his wife and family to go and live on this thing while waiting for a storm that they all said would never come.

"There was a growing gamble among the townspeople. How long they thought this would go on, this thing with the people on the carrier with his family and all those animals and birds sitting there waiting for it to rain, before he would have to give up, dismantle it and let everything go free.

The bets ranged anywhere from a week to a few days to over a month, to even a year before they either ran out of food or got stuck with a terrible case of cabin fever.

"The situation did produce one good thing. It united the townspeople. This being the one source of entertainment and the topic for their everyday conversation. After all, such a storm was unheard of in those days.

"But my people," Pebble continued, "were instrumental in the constructing of this project and keeping it together," said Pebble with a smirk.

"So, did it ever rain?" again asks Stan.

"Oh, yes it did," said Pebble, "when it finally started to rain, in about what seemed to be a few months or so after everyone settled into the carrier, the townsfolk stopped gathering around so much. The day it started to rain was just like every other day, bright and sunny with a slight breeze here and there. Once it started to rain though, boy, oh boy, did it rain.

"You see, after a while, most of the townspeople never really paid it much attention. They just went about their daily lives. But one day, it was in the middle of the day, the sun was about directly overhead, this bright sunshine soon gave way to a partly cloudy sky, and the wind picked up slightly. The dark clouds soon after descended over the entire area, and it seemed to turn daylight into night, much to the same effect of your hurricanes. This kind of occurrence happens all the time during the rainy season, and so when it is about to rain, no one paid much attention to it. It was just as it was during the rainy season. The dark clouds would come in, and they would last for days and days on end, even though it would rain for just a few hours before stopping and restarting again later, but that is during the rainy season. These dark clouds were darker than the ones seen before, and they were more condensed as if they would bring with them a lot more rain. For this storm, however, the dark clouds were followed by some loud thunder and bright flashes of lightning, in a somewhat violent sequence.

"Did this storm have a name?" asked Porter, "cause back home all of the terrible storms that we know have names, so we can identify them and refer to them later in life. Some are more dangerous than others, though. We rate the dangerous ones by placing them into numbered categories."

"No, this storm did not have a name, nor did it fit into any category. It was in a class all to itself. We did not name our storms," said Pebble.

"The old man just knew that this was coming and was to prepare for it somehow. Beyond that, all that there was out here were the wet and dry season and a cold and hot one," Pebble continued.

"So, you were telling us it started to rain. I am curious to see what happened next, said Porter, "so please continue."

'They say curiosity may have killed the cat, but I say a nine-life warranty brought him back," said Dae. "and I am curious to know what happened next as well."

"One hour of rain became several hours when it did start to rain, although several hours of rain was not unusual in that area in those days. Still, no one paid any attention to this, but then several hours became one day, then two days. Even up to this point, it did not cause for alarm, because the water level was not accumulating on any body of water to create any concern. It just rained, and the water just seemed to run off to wherever it usually ran off to, perhaps the rivers, lakes, streams, and the sea, or maybe it somehow got evaporated underground soon after that.

"By the time they got to the fourth day of the rain, however, it was unprecedented for it to rain for such a length of time continuously. The pace of the storm gradually picked up, coming down harder and in one general direction, straight down. Still, there was no massive flooding or panic after that very rough few first days. By the fifth day, however, the water level in the ponds around the area began to show signs of rising.

"Then a week came, and the water levels were now flooding over the areas where everyone walked and over everyone's farms. The small ponds that were few and far between were all joining together and becoming small lakes. The two or three rivers in the area soon began to have additional routes of water flowing. The single path where the water once flowed was now branching out, and new links were being added left and right along its way, due to the growing volume that was now flowing through them.

"Soon one week became two weeks, and things got nasty by the beginning of the second week. While it rained, the people started to come together after seeing the water level had risen steadily.

People could not open their doors, and in some cases, neighbors had to swim to get to each other's houses.

The rivers overran their banks and the sea which at first seemed so very far away, now joined the rivers. Soon you were not able to tell where the rivers ended, and the sea began. No one had to go out in boats to go fishing, the fishes came to them, right to their front doors in most cases. Sharks, alligators, and snakes all swam about right in front of houses and this became the new normal.

"It was now no longer possible to determine where the ponds, rivers and the ocean were. The different bodies of water did not have different colors as they once did. They all blended into each other creating a vast new body of water that no one could withstand.

There was water everywhere. Everything all around was raised, uprooted and most items started to float away, including the wooden carrier.

The townspeople came by, swimming, pounding on the side of the carrier wanting to be let in, but it was in vain. Once the doors were closed, they were not to reopen, and they could not open according to the old madman's claims about the instructions he had received.

"Surprisingly through all of this rain, the wind, even though it picked up slightly, was hardly noticed by anyone inside the carrier, and it was certainly nothing to cause the carrier to become unstable in any way. The carrier just floated away with the wind and water current."

"One of the old man's sons was heard to say he thought they were sailing in an east-northeast direction, although that was never confirmed or paid much attention to."

"The water that fell on the top of the carrier just ran off the sides.

It was so well built and put together with such good care, that nowhere did it leak, or accumulate water on the inside, and nowhere was it shaky, unstable, or uncomfortable.

"Even after all the banging on the sides and moving about of the people outside trying to get in, as well as all the animals on board, walking around, it remained stable. The debris passing along the sides, hitting it along the way, all of this abuse was not enough to cause any damage to its structure. This project so well assembled by my great-grandfather, cousins, and other family members, there was no way it was about to fall apart.

"A little after the second week of the continuous rain, the old man looked outside. He could see bodies floating around in the water, and what was left of the heads of the tall trees which he did not cut down. Some plant life that uprooted was also visible, and birds not chosen for the carrier were now landing on the roof of the carrier, but there was no way for them to enter it and nothing for them to eat.

"The situation was a desperate one. It seemed as though nothing would or could survive this weather without food and clean drinking water. Even the birds that remained had nowhere to land except on top of the carrier, but without food, they could only fly around for so long until fatigue would cause them to perish as well.

"All of the townspeople who were swimming around outside could only do so for so long. After all, they had nowhere to rest, and nothing to eat or drink. Eventually chronic fatigue took its toll on them, and their will to survive. Finally, they all gave up.

"Altogether it rained for forty days and forty nights nonstop and, unlike the rainy seasons it rained at a constant steady pace, straight down and very heavy. On the forty-first day, however, and without any warning, the rain stopped.

It was as if someone had turned on a water faucet and then suddenly turned it off.

Initially, the people inside did not know the rain had stopped. They just noticed that the carrier was no longer swinging back and forth as it once had.

It did not take long for word to get around that they had landed, but looking outside, they could see the water was still over a lot of areas, which would suggest that they landed on top of a hill or mountain or similar place.

"The old man would look every now and again outside to check out the situation and made sure it was okay to open the door. He knew according to the voices that the rain would stop on this day and time, but he kept that information to himself. It landed without causing a jolt of any kind. Such a smooth touchdown, not even his kids of their wives could have felt it. Soon the sun came out, and the speed with which the water was evaporating increased considerably.

"When it was all settled, the water subsided, and all that was left was a vast wasteland. They all knew everyone would have to start all over again. Everything and everyone not on the carrier now was gone.

"Suddenly there was a huge banging sound coming from the back of the carrier.

It was just the sound of the back of the carrier hitting the ground after the old man opened and lowered the back with his sons. Not waiting to be released, all the birds, one by one, began to fly out of the carrier and into the open air.

The animals heard that the birds had left, and they were free to go as well. One by one, they also began their migration to exit the carrier.

"The vegetation of the land was very sparse, but the old man assured his family that this would be enough to go around for all. There was some grass, but it was so low to the ground that the animals and birds had to step lightly to get the food they needed. The very slim pickings of plant life here and there suggested that this vegetation was new, perhaps coming about in the last few days before the carrier landed here, but there were no animals or other people around. Life as we know it had to start over again. You can see, your ancestors, the other rocks, had a major role to play in the building of this carrier," said Pebble. "So there is still a lot of good use in you."

"I am not sure when or where you were able to remove nails, or when we got away from using rocks to using metals, but it is nice to see how far we have come."

While Pebble was telling the story, he pointed to Roybe and said, "You see, you, too, are descendant of me; you also came from where we came. Everything that has to do with cutting or weaponry all started out with us, the rocks, and along the way, newer techniques were used and developed to keep up with the changing times." "So you, Swordan, you too are part of this distant bloodline, that common ancestry, as are you, Roybe. From using rocks as cutting objects to weapons, your and my ancestors used me and my people and their sharp edges to shave off the edges of the wood to get it into shape to make this large carrier, so you, too, should be proud of your past as well."

Swordan was a bit surprised to hear that what was used to make Roybe was at least similar to what was used to make him.

Feeling somewhat relieved now knowing that his past was more vibrant than he had previously thought, Stan finally smiled for the first time since he had gotten there and said, "Now I can go on, now we can go on. Thank you very much. I feel so much better now."

Looking around the vast wasteland that is now the desert, Walt asked turning to Pebble, "So where do you think are all those animals and plant life are now?"

"Since the rain stopped and the water subsided, the carrier did not resettle where it lifted from, so no one knows for sure where and when it settled, and some say that when the animals came off the carrier, they did not recognize the new place either. They all migrated to far off lands; some were carried off to new homes on ships.

"It's said that once these animals resettled in their new area, they too were never quite the same as they reproduced. New creatures were created, and with the new vegetation they had to eat, some of them looked very different than they did before, with varying shapes of bodies and features emerging.

"As far as the animals and people left behind, I am sure by now you have heard about the vultures, and what they do when they see some animal not moving," Pebble explained, "There were two vultures aboard the carrier."

"Yes, we have all heard about the vultures," said Walt.

"That is such a sad story," said Loepanda, as he sat down. "I think we should rest here for a while. I am so depressed right now."

Loepanda sat down and placed both his hands on his head, looking down. Even though they were not moving while Pebble was telling the story, he was still tired from being stationary. Everyone thought it was a good idea to sit and rest for a bit, but this would be more of a mental break, a chance to recoup after having to take in all that information.

"I, for one would like to hear a happier story," said Loepanda "Does anyone here know a happier story?" he asked, looking up. Since no one responded to Loepanda's challenge, he said, "Well, I have a few things I would like to say."

"You should relax and let everyone do the same," said Pebble to Loepanda.

Loepanda, looking at everyone but pointing to Pebble, said, "You see, that's the problem. I get no respect."

"So what do you call a grandfather rock that sits on the countertop?" asked Loepanda.

There was no response from anyone. They sat there as if to reinforce their claim that they were all way too tired to do anything, including think.

The lack of response did not deter Loepanda in any way; he just continued.

"You call it 'Gran night,'" he said, laughing, but he was the only one doing so.

"I thought you wanted to hear a happier story," said Pebble to Loepanda, "but it appears to me that you want to tell jokes instead."

"Yes, I do want to tell jokes," said Loepanda, "You tell stories, I tell jokes, that's how we get along," said the smiling Loepanda, "we need to liven up the place."

So Loepanda continued, "What do you call a small rock that ends up being a deadbeat like his father?"

Again no one answered. "A chip off the old block," he said.

Loepanda laughed although he knew he was the only one laughing again and, as he did this, he held his stomach and expanded and closed his tail.

"What did they name the little girl whose mother was sand and father was a rock?" Again no one answered. Up to this point, no one appeared to be much in the mood for jokes, and so Loepanda again continued, "Roxanne, they call her Roxanne." This time everyone else got it and laughed, that is, except Pebble, who did not show any expression while everyone else laughed at what he thought was at his expense.

Pebble had no jokes about Loepanda, so he just smiled and said, "I do not have any scorpion jokes, its like lawyer and doctor jokes, there are a million lawyer jokes and no doctor jokes."

Pebble then rolled over to where Loepanda was, Loepanda got very silent, as the smile quickly left his face. Pebble stood directly in front of him and looked down on him.

With Loepanda being only a quarter of Pebble's height, the shadow of Pebble completely covered him. Pebble tilted his head back and forth and side to side.

While Loepanda stood motionless, Pebble's shadow, with his movement at first covered Loepanda, then exposed him then it covered him again and moved away. Pebble then placed his hands on his hips, looked at Loepanda and smiled and asked, "So, how is the weather down there?" as all the tools exploded in laughter at Loepanda.

Loepanda, now that he was all out of smart remarks, just rolled his tail up and sat back down, not making another rock comment after that.

For the most part, the remainder of the day just seemed to drag on without much of anything happening.

Although the day appeared to be a long one, no one was complaining about being hungry or physically tired. It was more of emotional tiredness. Tiredness filled with the tools talking about the things they had built or wanted to create in their lifetime.

The tools that are battery operated, who by now should be out of energy, and want to recharge, did not mention it. They had plenty of life left, despite not knowing how long they would be out here.

The sun was now directly overhead, bearing down hard on them, and by the feel of it, they assumed the temperature had reached the high for the day. It was going to be a long time before evening hit and the cooling started.

Things were so quiet that, in fact, Pebble and Loepanda now sat next to each other and neither one was upset or angry with the other. It was as though both had reconciled their differences and were now just sitting there enjoying each other's company. What they were talking about, if anything, was not directly heard by the others.

"You know right about now I could go for a game of Phzed," said Porter, Everyone looked at him and started laughing.

"You are two croutons short of a salad," said Walt, "and there is a problem. "We do not have a dice."

"What's a dice?" asked Pebble.

"It is a hard substance like a rock, but it is even on all sides, and on each of its sides it has a number that ranges from one to six, and its corresponding number on the other side add up to seven," said Dae.

"You know it is my church, we could make a dice," said Porter. "I mean we have plenty of rocks lying around here and I am sure with the right tool meaning us together, we could chip the edges off these rocks, then carve numbers into the sides of them and have ourselves a nice smooth dice to play with," said Porter.

"What are we going to use to write with on these rocks?" asked Roybe.

"Perhaps I could help," said Swordan. "I could carve or scratch numbers into the sides of the rocks."

"Or perhaps I can help as well," said Ariel.

"And how do you play this game?" asked Loepanda.

"Well, that I can explain," said Porter.

Porter began to explain the game to Loepanda and Pebble. After some more discussion, there was a general agreement among everyone that it would be too time-consuming and too much trouble to try and build a dice from rock and having to explain this game to everybody else. The decision was this was not the time or place to try to create the game or play any games.

It was now late afternoon perhaps about 16:30.

The tools still sat, none of them sure what they were waiting for or who they were waiting for. Everyone was resting, although still, no one was physically tired.

"So where do you go on from here?" Loepanda asked Pebble.

"I am not particularly sure," Pebble responded. "I have been lingering around this area for so long, I think the past couple hundred years, so I guess that I will relax here for the time being," said Pebble. "Perhaps I will hang around here until the next massive rainstorm comes around and brings some much-needed vegetation back to this once fertile land. I think I will walk around here looking pretty," said Pebble.

"Well you are going to be doing a lot of walking," said Loepanda.

"But I am not going to hold my breath for any drastic changes."

"Life is way too short. You either get busy going with the flow, or you're too busy to notice that there is a flow. I have seen this place stay pretty much the same for the past couple hundred years. Although I could say, I never expected to find your tools out here in my lifetime. You tools from the future wandering around out here, this was something unexpected," said Pebble.

"Perhaps the next set of whatever I encounter would be my close friends, and we would do things together besides sitting around telling stories about the past," Pebble continued.

"A change of scenery would be nice for me, though," said Loepanda. Every generation should not have the same scenery as the one before. We should keep on growing and keep on changing."

None of the other tools joined in on Pebble's and Loepanda's discussion. They just listened and drifted off in their little world, not paying any attention to what either one had to say.

"Change in this land is hard to come by. It's like watching the shorthand on the clock. Sure it does move, but anyone does not notice it. That is the way it is here on the dune. With each gust of wind, some sand runs off the top and sides and reshapes the dunes, but it is such a slight change, no one notices it until they have moved away and return," said Pebble.

AQUALYN

"Hello, hello, you folks out there, how are you guys doing?" was the strange voice heard coming from a distance, and it was also an echo, so no one was quite sure which direction it was coming. Everyone got to their feet and looked out and around to see who was calling out to them.

When Loepanda had arrived, the ground was shaking. When they met Pebble, it was a surprise to all of them that they had not noticed him before, but with this new visitor, the wind and dust picked up and grew stronger as he approached. It was as if he had arrived with the wind.

Another visitor came by, this time a canteen just passing through, dressed in what would become his trademark green camouflage with black stripes. He was a round man about ten inches in circumference and had a long leather strap about eighteen inches long hanging from his head. He approached the tools and stood in front of them with his hands on his hip, and sticking his tongue out like a dog that is either very thirsty, out of breath or in desperate need to have some water.

Porter turned to him and asked, "Well, who on earth are you?"

"I am thirsty, but that is not my name, but it is all you need to know right now, and I am dying of thirst and going insane," the canteen responded.

'Lordy, I'd say you are two ice cubes short of a slushy," said Porter.

With everyone's attention now apparently on the canteen, he looked at them and asked, "Does anyone know where I can get a refill? My reserve is empty and you don't need to know the details."

Porter, Roybe, and Walt looked at each other with a combination of not knowing the answer and surprise as to what was asked of them. They then looked at the canteen again as they all shook their heads to say no.

"I am so sorry," said the canteen as he extended his hands to shake the hands of first Porter and then Walt. "Allow me to introduce myself. Aqualyn is the name. Supplying water to all is for what I am famed."

"Supplying water you say, but you seem to be the one needing water right now, said Porter.

"For that my friend is correct. You are the smart one, should I bet, said Aqualyn.

"I am hoping you can show or point me in the direction of some of it.

Make it nice and crisp, because quite a bit I have to fit," Aqualyn continued.

Brin looked at Aqualyn and asked, "Shouldn't we be the ones asking you where the water is?"

"How much water are you looking for and how and where did you get to water the last time you were empty?" Brin continued.

"The last time I had some water, one of your buds over there dug a hole for me, and I was so impressed with the work he had done, I named this hole my little sea," Aqualyn said, pointing to Dae.

Dae noticed right at the beginning, when he first heard Aqualyn speak, that Aqualyn had a unique way of phrasing things. Every sentence he uttered flowed to another poetically, but Dae said nothing at first, only listening as Aqualyn explained things to the others.

Just to prove it or at least test his theory, Dae thought he should ask Aqualyn a question so he could listen to his answer. "So how deep a hole did my friend dig up for you?" Dae asked. Dae moved in closer to Aqualyn to listen carefully to his answer.

"He dug a water hole so wide and deep, and it supplied water for everyone to use and keep. But that was so very long ago; the wind has since covered that water hole back up you know."

Dae smiled to himself, knowing, like always, he was right, and not only was he right, he was also the only one to notice the poetic nature of Aqualyn's comments.

"How long did it take them to dig that hole the last time?" Dae asked again.

"It took them about 40 days of nonstop sweat and toil, but in the end, we knew it was water we would find beneath the soil," replied Aqualyn.

"And let me guess, it took 40 nights as well," asked Loepanda, as everyone erupted in laughter, that got everyone laughing except Aqualyn, of course, who either did not see the humor or he did not get the joke.

"You would have to have been with us for a while to understand why that was so funny," said Porter.

"Is it me or does everything around here take around 40 days and 40 nights to be accomplished?" asked Loepanda.

"Well, everything does not take that long to get done. I can recall the last job that took that long and then some," said Aqualyn.

"I have been walking now for so long, I have somehow lost track of time, the distance I have traveled through both rain and bright sunshine. I was on a project that seemed to take more like 40 years to get done. This included materials that weigh more than a ton. It is from there, that far off place from which I come, through the wind and rain and the blazing sun."

As Aqualyn was telling the tales of his travels, he used his hands a lot in open form and pointed to the tools to relay what he was saying.

"The idea for it had been around for a long, long time, a wild and crazy idea that once it was built somehow, one day, it would shine," said Aqualyn.

"Oh, a wild and crazy idea. We have had our fill of hearing about wild and crazy things, so go ahead and try to surprise us," said Ed.

"So where exactly did you walk from?" Brin turned to Aqualyn and asked.

"Well, I have been walking this way now for the past 18 years, and it has all been in one direction like going down a slope of stairs. It has taken me that long to get to this place, but rest assured now that I am here, I will be on the case. At my last project, I met some of your folks, but they were much bigger and made of different strokes," said Aqualyn, pointing to Pebble.

"They were at least a thousand times larger than you are, and very well educated and well-mannered by far. They were on a mission and did not let anything get in their way, no matter how few they were or what anyone had to say."

"Oh, finally, a happier tale," said Porter, as he got up and started to clap his hands.

"Yes, indeed, this does sound like a much happier story," said Kati, "I love those."

Everyone got excited and came in a little closer to Aqualyn to hear his tale about his travels. Porter turned to Aqualyn and commented, "I hope this is not another story about just the rocks. We have all heard about them and what they have done, how much they have contributed to the past, and we are so happy for them.

"You are talking about big and sturdy rocks, but back, where I come from we have buildings made out of stone. We call them skyscrapers. They are huge rock-like objects that stand in the middle of our cities," said Ed.

The excitement was growing as everyone now was anxious to hear the tale of these rocks that are bigger than anything they have seen or heard.

Up to this point, the most prominent rocks known to them were the anchor rocks used on the rainy-day project, and in Aqualyn's tales and description, these rocks seemed in some way to be different, they looked purpose-driven or at least educated.

"It's my church in the past that all the tools that were around in the region at the time were either made of rocks or wood," said Porter.

"Out of curiosity, were these used as tools?" asked Pebble.

But before Aqualyn could answer, Walt, interrupted with, "were they being used as a fastener to hold something together, or were they being used to hold something down, or in place?"

"Wow, wow, wow, please one at a time," said Aqualyn, as he held his hands up in a gesture for them to stop shooting off questions that rapidly.

"Not having the chance to answer all is a crime. This I can avoid if you'd give me time."

These rocks were huge, and they well carved,

And if there was a drought, you know they will not starve.

There was nothing like them anywhere else around,

And when they performed together, there was no prettier sound.

They were well educated and formed themselves into shapes,

Perfect rectangles equal in size like drapes," Aqualyn continued.

As Aqualyn was reading on about the rocks, the tools' heads would tilt left and right and as Aqualyn started a new sentence, each new sentence got an "ooh" and "ahhhh" at the end.

Dae just listened without comment or moving his head in any way.

Aqualyn's way of telling the story got the same response as if Dae was saying it. It captivated them, although no one was sure why. There was a lot of excitement, you could see it their eyes, as they sat upright looking him directly in the face eager to hear more.

"Please, please tell us more about these rocks," said Loepanda.

"Patience, patience is a virtue, my friend. I will tell you more, as the story transcends," said Aqualyn.

Aqualyn began again where his story had left off. "Well for years, everyone would wonder what time of the day it was, as the rumor of lunch and dinner would cause such a buzz.

They needed to know so they could plan prayers and meals, and if someone got sick, how long it would take to heal.

But there was no way of knowing time, date or the given day; they just listened to whatever the elders had to say.

All we knew was when morning started, they ate some food, and the dew departed.

In the middle of the morning when our stomach fights the roar, a bite and a drink would sure settle the score. This is the time when some people call brunch, not a big a meal like what we call lunch.

And when the evening began, we ate once more, before going to sleep and closing our doors.

Somewhere in the middle of the day, we would eat again; perhaps we would kill a goat or the neighbor's hen.

There was always someone to tell you when each function would take place, like the one at our meal, who would say all the grace.

And it was always a different person saying it each time, who knew if they got everything or they left some behind.

All we know is, that we ate when we were hungry, and drank when we were thirsty, we knew when water was close, by the sound of the birdie, but time was never of the essence, as long as good food was in our presence.

My job function in conjunction was to supply water as needed, and this I did with grace, and it is how I succeeded.

When it was time to drink, there was no time to sit and think, and that's what I always did, while my fatigue I hid.

"So tell us, what was near these rocks?" asked Ed.

"Next to this river, this vast river and where my last water fills up became my dinner, is where these rocks were. On this fertile ground, is the perfect setting for a king to be crowned.

"This water was cold, and it flowed with no ripple, and when it would rain, its flow would then triple. Except for a little rush, here and again, just a steady slow flow, until it reached its end. Its very end was not much to see, but it impressed everyone, this includes me, as it went along the way, both night and day.

There are these cliffs next to a large river that had rocks that were white, and they presented a view, that from afar was a delight.

They had no particular formation but provided the eye with quite the stimulation.

Everyone would look on in ahhhh, and ohhhhh.

It was like a performance where no one would boo.

Well the rocks formed themselves out of these white rocks that took years and years, they took pride in their work and carried on it with care, to create these building blocks, there was no set time as to when they did start.

But each one did pitch in to do their fair part.

But the thing that is amazing was that real crazy part.

How these rocks came together to form such a work of art.

Legend has a theory as to how they got to their final place, but that was never proven, it is not an open/shut case.

Some say they rolled over and over to their permanent spot, landed in a place with timing on the dot.

Legend also has it that several giant birds came down from the sky, perhaps vultures or eagles, or a giant house fly. And they were saddened by these rocks lying dead, and stood them upright, to what became their permanent bed.

But these are just tales of this legend I hate to doubt because I am polite, and I would have no clout.

But I think they used smaller rocks to roll these rocks along, and it did move along smoothly like a beautiful song.

These rocks were also talented in the way they could play; folks gathered from far and nearby they say.

The sound of different musical instruments they would play day and night, and different groups of people from all over they would unite.

But the wind would blow through and also around them; the sound was music to the ear of everyone a, godsend.

They were the celebrities of their day and time, and at night under the stars, they would shine.

They would give off a glow that was seen for miles away, and away from this event, no one could stay.

Everyone would gather to hear the wind in the trees whistle, and the flow of the water in the river bristle.

But the rocks were always the main attraction; they were the stars, who provided all the action."

"For how long these rocks would perform?" Dae then asked.

"Usually for about two hours or so, it has been known to go longer though," Aqualyn replied.

"When these rocks were performing, did you have to provide them with water?" asked Roybe.

"No, I did not, I'd give them all I got, you see I missed my shot, but I am sure if I had to, I'd do it in a hurry, even though outside I knew it was hot.

I am sure if that is what they wanted, I will surely fit the bill.

And remain on the case until the rocks had their fill."

Before Aqualyn came about, no one had ever captured the tools' attention like Dae; no one was falling asleep or wandering off somewhere or letting their minds drift away.

"Yes, listening to Aqualyn was like listening to music. It captivated them more and more as he spoke.

Aqualyn went on to say, "These rocks one day after performing for a huge crowd did something we thought should have never been allowed.

They quietly went out into the fields and did not move, each with the memory of the performance still fresh in its groove.

There they supported each other and carried each other along, just as they did when they performed their songs.

By picking up the weak ones and place them on their heads, holding them straight as if they were dead.

When they came to a stop, with the weak ones on top, they interlocked on each other's heads, so no one rock carried the weight it is said.

There were quite a few about five dozens.

Some brothers and sisters, some close friends and cousins.

I left them there and went away for a while, sticking around for a long time was not my style.

Time went by so fast, we all changed, we moved on. I kept thinking I will return only to find them all gone.

The landscape had changed the grass all grown.

The scenery is different, its age now showed."

"How long were you away from these rocks?" asked Walt.

"We had no way of knowing and of measuring time, what I recall is from memory those memories are all mine.

But it seems I was away for only a while, and I did not go far, perhaps just a mile.

Then one day, one winter I came back around, to the place where I left them, that was now sacred ground.

People now gather to worship and pray, but they cannot stay all night, this is not okay.

And there they stood tall, all of them so proud of their stance.

I knew this, in an instant, no long stare, just a glance.

I often said if I ran into them still standing out there, I would walk up and say hello, it would only be fair, in the middle of the field, in a perfect form, was where they stood and weathered the storm.

In my mind, I did go and visit and catch one last performance even if I had no ticket.

I spent the whole day with them catching up on the past.

Why it seemed like yesterday, boy how time went by so fast!

We laughed, and we talked about the good old days.

And the things we remembered. I was amazed.

The next day when the sun was directly overhead, and a brisk wind came by, I knew they were alive, and not dead.

And their shadows were directly under them at this time. I knew it was once again their moment to shine.

I saw people around them who would gather and pray, although it was clear they knew just what they had to say.

When the wind would blow through them, the sound was a gem, and the dust cloud was created, I stay all day, for them I waited.

They played before having their meals and leaving their homes each day, the next day this was repeated as it was day after day.

As the sun moved farther west, you see the shadow moving slowly as well, you knew the day was aging, by the wind you could tell.

At last check, these rocks were so old, and they have since turned to gray, but you knew that by each other's side forever they would stay.

And gravity has taken its toll on their place.

Soon once again this will become open space.

They are now beginning to sink into the ground, slowly but surely without making a sound.

And the rocks that were to hold and carry the weaker ones on their heads, they have now relied on each other as their bed. They have gotten weak and frail over time, but together they stay through rain and sunshine.

Although today some of them are still standing tall, through good and bad times they have been through it all.

It is not clear what will happen to them in time to come, but one thing is sure, they will change some.

As severe weather and shifts in the earth, takes its toll, for sure, but one thing is sure they will endure.

As I just left them and headed southeast, this is my journey, the nature of my beast.

And that is why I ended up here, guys, this is my story, all truths no lies, said Auqalyn.

He captured their attention as no one did before. "Do these rocks or the area where they are, have a name?" asked Dae.

"You know, I had the same question," said Stan.

Yes, me too, me three, me four, and so on said the other tools.

"Yes, it does have a name, and they kept it simple, no guessing game.

Stonehenge was the name of the place of these rocks, all belonging to the same flock.

My only hope is for you, my friend Dae, for you to be so kind as to dig me a hole, please. Please say yea or nay, dig it far and deep until you hit the water, it would make me happy, I could save lives for when it got hotter.

I can refill my body and continue my way, as well as provide you with water, should you need it night or day," said Aqualyn.

Everyone was tired already just from being in the sun for so long, and the fatigue made them not want to go on anywhere.

Right about now, they could all use some recharging. If only there were an electrical outlet for them to do so, or perhaps they could all use some water.

Perhaps resting here for the night and continuing in the morning would be a great idea. It did not occur to anyone that they had not moved a foot since Aqualyn began to tell his story, or from the spot where they heard about the rainy-day project.

"I feel as though my battery is winding down, my energy level is dropping very quickly," said Walt. "I think my battery will die if we continue any farther without me shutting down for the evening, or at least for a while. My energy will get depleted as well," he continued.

"Believe you me, I feel the same way," said Porter.

"But you don't have a battery," said Ed to Porter.

"I know, but I still feel like I should be resting for the evening," said Porter.

"We should camp here for the night, and power down these tools." We cannot run all day and all night on these batteries. We will not have any energy in the morning, a few hours at the most," Porter continued.

The tools nodded and agreed that they should indeed rest for the evening and build another fire bright and early in the morning. Then continue along their way, wherever that may lead if they moved at all.

"So how and where do you intend to find this water?" asked Ed.

"I don't know, I don't know, but when we get there, the signs they will show," Aqualyn responded.

"I am not sure," said Ed. "we have seen a lot of this place, and all I can see is desert, sand and more deserts. I am not sure what signs you will be looking for to find water," he continued.

The evening was fast approaching, it was about two hours later, about 18:30, and as they had the previous evening, they dug a small hole, and gathered up all the little pieces of brush and whatever they could find along the way.

Unlike the previous night, however, tonight Pebble suggested that they gather up some of the small rocks in the area and include them in the making of the fire. This was after in a conversation with Dae, in which he told Dae that stones could keep the heat longer than the wood and bones could ever do.

Pebble had a different whistle; it was one that only the other rocks in the area could hear and understand. It was their unique language or dialect spoken by their people alone. When he whistled, a few of the little rocks in the area ran over to him and wanted to be part of the fire.

The rocks came over, and there was no introduction given or needed to each other. Pebble felt that there was no need. There were small and large rocks, and they piled onto each other to start the fire.

They camped for the night with no one saying much about anything for the remainder of the evening. The strange thing about the tools now was the fact that no one said anything about missing their home, this despite the fact that it seemed like days since they had been away from it.

No one had any sadder stories about being out here and not being able to use their talents, or of not being around their friends. Having Pebble and Aqualyn come along and share their stories, all the sadness seemed to have disappeared. Now all that remained was a severe case of fatigue and the wanting to know more.

Before going to bed, there were no bedtime stories or reflections on the day's events, there were not even any good nights or "see you in the morning," it was just silence before they all fell asleep.

The next day, the sun came up again, and this day it seemed to come down harder on the land than the day before, but it also appeared to do so earlier. The dry air was a bit much for a lot of them to handle so early in the morning, but no one did or said anything about it. Unlike the previous morning where they were all were stiff and had to stretch to get going, today that did not seem to be the case.

Loepanda said to the tools, "All of you working out here and being without any water or any form of lubrication will eventually get thirsty and tired, and this will lead to dehydration and a general breakdown of your parts. No man is a desert, and you will be in desperate need for some lubrication, so I think that we should all pool our resources and find a spot to camp and get some much-needed water. We will need it for when and if we are to continue along in the hot boiling sun," Loepanda continued.

"Wow, you sound just like Dae," said Ed to Loepanda.

Aqualyn turned to them and said, "When we get hungry and thirsty and feel all alone, we can't see ourselves having dinner from a menu of stone. The one comfort we will have will be that of a drink so our stomachs could have something, and our minds could think."

"Why did the rocks select that particular spot to rest and why did they decide not to go on any farther?" Stan asked Aqualyn.

"This spot seems like a perfect place to be; after all, they were not too far away from their family, and the sea.

"They just decided it was time to end. It was time to leave all future performing to a new breed; it was their time to call it a day, you could tell by their yawning and to let other stars shine and take the spotlight, have someone else succeed."

"They decided that since they had set the tone for everyone else to follow, they had established a system for measuring time, it was smooth and shallow, and telling what time of the day specified things were to be done, either morning or evening, under the stars or sun.

"So they figured their jobs were now complete, and they should end up on top before something brings about their defeat."

"That is kind of like the way we were in the shed," said Dae. "One day we are all in there together, the next day, one of us gets broken, and replaced with another tool, something smaller and faster. Another tool can perform multiple functions, and before you know it, we all look back on our lives and ask, "What have we contributed to society? "What will they remember us for?" "What have we done with our lives?" and "What are we passing on to the next generation, our children and their children?" These are the questions we seek answers to, and we must ask of ourselves. I for one do not want to be remembered for what I have done, but for what we as a team have accomplished. I know we have accomplished great things, and we will continue to accomplish great things in the future if we work together. As one, we can build a seat for someone to sit on, but as a group, we can build a stadium for everyone to sit and watch those rock stars perform." As Dae ended his statement, he opened his hands as if to welcome comments.

There was no comment. No one had anything further to add, and as usual no one challenged Dae, but also no one ever has anything to add to one of Dae's statements that can make it better in any way. For they all knew that they could not sound more intelligent or improve anything upon that he has said.

Although Aqualyn comes close, he does not have the same connection with the tools as Dae.

Dae looked at Aqualyn and said, "Okay, I will do it, I will help to dig you a hole to find water because I am sure the day will come when not only I will need water, but we as a group will as well. I would not like to think that I had the opportunity to do something and did not act on it. Opportunities will knock, but only once at our door.

Besides, who knows what we will encounter tomorrow or the day after. We may need the water then. There is nothing worse than for a man to look back on his life and wonder in regret. There is no more significant failure than having your enemies thinking that they were correct," said Dae.

Loepanda extended his tail and said, "Let me help as well. I can sense where we might be able to find water," Loepanda, facing the tools, extended his tail and rolled it back up again.

The tools were not aware of what Loepanda was trying to do or say at first, but he was smiling as he was rolling his tail back and forth and then he would sink his tail into the ground, pull it out and say "No, not here." He then ran a little farther out, first ten then 20 feet, stopped again and again and said, "Nope, not here either."

"What in the world are you doing?" asked Porter.

"I am trying to find where the water will be. I am sticking my tail into the ground to see where the sand is most moist," responded Loepanda.

"Well, if this continues all day, it will make it seem as though we have been here for 40 days and 40 nights. Surely there has got to be a better way to find water than this primitive method," said Porter, looking at Loepanda running around and sticking his tail into the sand here and there.

"Perhaps we should look somewhere else, a spot where the earth has sunken in, or maybe a region where we see some sign of vegetation, a palm tree or a cactus," said Swordan, as Loepanda continued to run around, sticking his tail into the sand.

"Look around you here," said Pebble," Where do you see vegetation anywhere? I think we should let Loepanda continue to do its thing, and try to find us some water, after all, he knows this terrain better than any of us."

They watched the spectacle of Loepanda running around for a few more minutes when all of a sudden he stopped.

Loepanda paused for a brief moment, turned to the tools and said "You know, like I said, my tail is a radar. I can find water; I can sense water, I can tell you exactly where this water is located."

"Well, did you find any water?" asked Ed.

"No," said Loepanda. "I just wanted to stop and tell you guys that. I just wanted to make sure you were still watching and waiting for me. I have to search a little farther."

This continued for another ten minutes, with Loepanda going from spot to spot trying to find water until he finally he stopped again.

He stared at the tools silently as if he was about to make an announcement.

"You know, you should never cry wolf," said Ed.

"When he stopped this time, Loepanda had one more parting shot to take at Pebble, before admitting to the crowd that he had indeed found where the water would be, or at least found where he thought water would be.

"What do you call rocks that stand on a stage, kicking their feet in the air to music? "He paused and opened his arms awaiting an answer. No one knew the answer or wanted to play any more games, as Loepanda started to laugh to himself.

"Okay you guys give up?" he asked. This time, Pebble started laughing as well. Pebble, however, rolled over to where Loepanda was laughing and pointed at Loepanda.

Everyone looked on as the Pebble approached Loepanda. Loepanda was not sure why Pebble was laughing at his joke, as he walked over to him. Loepanda thought that Pebble was about to hurt him in some way or perhaps crush him, but instead, he approached and said, "Ha, ha, ha, I know that one. "You call them the rockets!" said Pebble as he laughed along with Loepanda and everyone else joined as well.

Loepanda, not wanting to be upstaged by Pebble, changed the subject (and he also did not want anyone to pay any attention to what the rock just said) so he yelled out, "FOUND IT."

"Did you really?" asked Pebble.

"Yes I did," replied Loepanda.

"It is here, it is right here," said Loepanda, almost as if he were singing it. He would punch his tail into the ground then pull it out, then stick it into the ground again. He did this while he is dancing around each time, singing, "It is here, it is here, it is here, it is right here."

The tools all gathered closer to where Loepanda and Pebble were standing.

"Where, where can we start digging?" asked Dae.

With its face to the tools, and its tail into the ground, he said, "We could dig here. Then he pulled his tail out and stuck it back into the ground again a little farther away and said, "We can dig here, too."

He repeated this for about five or six times. He would take his tail out, move a little farther away; stick it back into the ground, to show that what he was referring to was all around him.

Everyone was anxious to start digging, but before they could begin, Dae held up his hand and said, "Wait we need to formulate a plan."

"Why would we need a plan to dig? You see sand, you remove it," said Loepanda. "It is not that complicated."

There was silence throughout the area and a look of shock. For the first time in everyone's memory, this was the first time anyone had ever questioned what Dae had to say, or what he just said.

This was beyond anything that any of them had heard before. They stood around with their jaws dropped, and no one dared to utter as much as a whisper. Everyone stood there and looked at Loepanda as Loepanda looked back at them, not sure what was wrong, or even aware that he had done something wrong.

He stood there with a blank look on his face, looking at the tools and asked, "What, did I say or do wrong?"

Dae just cleared his throat and looked at Loepanda. Loepanda began to step back slowly. As he did so, he would lower himself to the ground. He felt the same way he felt when Pebble was approaching him, scared about what he thought was about to happen.

Dae did not yell or raise his voice to Loepanda in protest or retaliation. Dae just looked at him and smiled and repeated what he had said before, that they should formulate a plan.

"Where was the center of where the water found?" Dae asked Loepanda.

He stood up slowly and said, "It was here." He moved away a little from Dae and stuck his tail into the ground again, expressionless, and repeated his claim, "it is also here," pointing to another spot about one foot away.

"Okay then, since this is the center of where the water found, and it was said to be over there and over here as well, we should spread out over this area and dig in teams," said Dae.

As Dae said this, he moved his hands outward to gesture for everyone to spread out and form a circle, "Here is what we are going to do. We will select numbers, one through one hundred, and the one closest to whatever number I choose will be the one that goes first.

When someone digs, he should grab the dirt and move it out of the way. While he is out of the way, his buddy will come in behind him and do the same thing. When that person goes in and digs up some dirt, comes out and throws it out onto the banks, we will then determine how much dirt he picked up and how long it took them to drop it off and return and get some more dirt. Whoever goes in behind them has to do likewise in time and quantity. We will do this until we reach the water," Dae continued.

Dae went in first to show how he thought the digging should be.

He dug up some dirt, three-quarters of a shovel full, walked back about 20 feet, dumped it and came back for more.

"Let me try it," said Swordan, as he too dug up some dirt, but instead of walking back with it and dumping it far away, as instructed by Dae, he threw it over his shoulder, and it went to the same place where Dae had walked to and placed his dirt.

"That, too, will work," said Dae, referring to where and how Swordan threw the sand.

"Yes, we will work in teams. If one team member fails to deliver the same result as the person before him, then his teammate has to make up for it in both time and volume, everyone agrees?" asked Dae.

Everyone nodded their heads to say yes, they did agree.

Brin, wanting to demonstrate he too could do something, dragged the sand out from where the center was to where Dae had placed his dirt.

This appeared to be a much lengthier process, and he took less sand away than did Swordan or Dae.

But needless to say, it got the job done, and Brin was able to come back and get some more sand and repeat the process all over again within the same period as did Dae and Swordan.

"I've cleared away lots of dirt in my lifetime, as did my family. We have always used to clearing away debris, brushing away dust and preparing ancient archeologist sites for cleaning, I've been doing this," said Brin. No one had an issue with the amount of sand Brin was clearing, as his timing was up to par.

Porter, realizing he would drag a lot less dirt that Brin, and not sure what he could do to help said, "Well guys, just let me know how I can help. Just somebody tells me what you need me to do."

As for Roybe, he was in the same boat as Porter, so he said to the group, "Well guys, I am here for you as well. Just let me know where I am needed and what I have to do."

"I think you could do the same as Brin did," said Dae.

"You have a long blade, and you are fast, all you have to do is to stick your blade into the sand and drag the sand all the way back out onto the banks," said Dae to Roybe.

"Okay, then that is what I will do," replied Roybe.

Dae suggested to the tools that could not help at that point that they should stand there and look on and cheer them on, or with the likes of Walt, Porter, and Ed, three or four of them could work together. Dae also suggested that the tools not in use at any given time would come in and fill up the slack for the tools that were falling behind. In some cases, if the sand should start to roll back down into the hole, other tools like Ed, Porter, Walt, and Kati or any other tool that was not in use, would take action. They would do this by sticking themselves into the ground along with some of the rocks around and be somewhat of a barrier or stake in the sand to prevent further erosion.

"Lordy, you mean be like the guys building the roads back home, where it takes two or three to do the work and the rest just to watch?" said Porter.

Everyone laughed at Porters analysis.

"There are two kinds of tools in this world, those that do the work and those that lie around and wait for work," said Ed. "I just never thought of myself as being part of the latter."

Pebble and Loepanda put their hands around each other and patted each other on the back.

"Let's do it," said Walt. "Let's get this done," as they gathered around and started to dig.

"Yes, let's work together," said Loepanda.

With the help of all the tools digging for several minutes, the pace was brisk and sometimes furious. Everyone would dig and return to the hole in the allocated time. It was if no one wanted to be an anchor and drag everyone else down, or perhaps they felt as if they were running out of time to get this hole done. Even though they were all thirsty and somewhat tired, they worked as if they were on a mission and time was their enemy.

The constant cheering on by the other tools that sat on the sidelines also helped along the way. It kept everyone motivated to work faster and harder and in a good mood. No one wanted to take a break or rest, for fear of and not wanting to be responsible for all f them falling behind.

Digging away and not paying attention to anything else, Dae came across a hard object buried deep in the ground. As his blade hit the object the first time, he paused and stopped digging for a moment. Dae held his hands up like a military commander would do to halt his men from advancing first folded.

Everyone stopped as instructed by Dae. The discovery of this object caught them by surprise, although no one at first saw it or knew what it was. The sound of the hard object did not cause any celebrations because it did not sound like water, but it was reason enough to bring all the work to a halt.

"I know that sound," said Dae, as if it was a sound he had heard played before.

He dug again, and hit the object once more, "I do recognize this sound, and let me tell you this, it is not the sound of water," said Dae.

"Let me get in there," said Swordan, as he got to where Dae was and started to dig as well, hitting the object a few times in the process as the sound played on.

The sound of Swordan's blade and the music of Dae hitting against the object were two completely different sounds. Everyone loved the sound it made when Dae struck it. When Swordan did the same thing, it was so bland, and it got no response. The other tools were not as impressed by the sound from Swordan hitting the object, but when Dae did it, it was music to their ears.

"Hit it again, Dae," said Porter.

"Perhaps Brin could clear away this area better than any of us so we can get a better view," said Dae.

"Good idea," said Brin, who then came over to where Swordan and Dae were standing and proceeded to clear away the area. As Brin began to brush away the field, it slowly came into view, and everyone else could see that it was that of yet another rock.

"Lordy, what is it with all these rocks all over the place?" asked Porter. "It seems as though every time I turn around, there is another rock coming out of the woodworks. Do rocks come out of the woodworks? Hmmm, surely not from where I stood," said Loepanda. If I had to guess from where they came, I'd spend all day thinking and end up insane," he continued.

Brin continued to brush around the outside, and soon he discovered that it appeared to be not only one rock but that of two rocks on top of each other.

Brin did not immediately announce that it was two rocks. From his point of view, he could see this, but all Dae and Swordan knew was that it was a hard object, and not necessarily two of them.

"If this is water, it is tough water," said Swordan.

"But it is way too hot down here for water to be frozen for so long.

Now that he was aware that they had discovered rock and not water, Dae suggested that they continue to clear around the stone by removing all the sand on top of it and around the edges. This clearing away was done by Dae and Brin, while the others just looked on patiently waiting.

"For the likes of me, I cannot understand why we are digging around a rock to find water," said Ed. "If you guys should at any time need some help from us, please let us know," Ed continued.

After several minutes of clearing, Dae came to realize as well that it was two rocks and not one as he thought and up until now only Brin had been aware of it.

The two rocks were of different colors, but they were both square, and flat.

The rock on top was a dark green-looking color, while the one on the bottom was a much darker black rock. The shadow of everyone standing over these rocks made it look like both rocks were of the same color.

Questions abounded in the minds of Dae and Brin as to how these rocks got here, who brought them here and why, but for now the immediate issue was the removal of these rocks so they could find the water they were searching.

The one that had not done or said much of anything for some time was Kati, who suddenly came over and said, "I want to help, and I would like to work with Brin," from here on out."

As much of a surprise as if was to hear Kati speak, it was hardly noticed by any of the tools, except for Dae, that Kati was silent for so long except for uttering a few words here and there earlier on.

"Well, we will need everyone's help in removing this rock," said Dae. "Come along, everyone," he said as he hand gestured for everyone that was sitting on the sidelines to come over to him.

Although both Dae and Brin knew it was two rocks and not one, the way they placed on top of each other so flat and dark. Brin had now cleared away enough of the dirt around the edges of the bottom rock to where they could get their hands under at least part of the foundation to get it lifted. Dae thought to himself that perhaps with everyone's help, they could remove both rocks at the same time.

Perhaps the other tools were color blind, or the shadow casts made both dark green and black rock look like one rock, whatever the reason the others were still unaware that it was two.

With everyone down to the rocks' base and trying to pry them upright, it was fruitless. Their first and second attempts were useless it soon became apparent by the way they were going about it. Trying to remove these two was not the right way to do it, they were too heavy. Trying to lift any of the rocks was no easy task, and they were trying to raise both at once, which appeared impossible.

"You know, on second thought, I think we should remove the top green one first, and then try for the second," said Dae.

The other tools standing around the outside were now also aware that it was two and not one.

"Lordy, you mean to tell that there are two of them?" asked Porter.

"Yes, there are two of them, one on top of the other, so let's try to remove the top one first and then the second," said Dae.

The shadows of the other tools were still covering the rocks. From this point on Dae thought Walt, Ed, and Porter could help, although he never specified in what capacity. Porter and Ed are two of those tools that needed to be explicitly told what their function is, or what exactly what they needed to do.

Both rocks were so tightly placed on top of each other, that Dae suggested Porter and Ed could be used to wedge themselves between the rocks and create a little opening so the others could get a better grip.

Once the rocks shifted, they could then get into between the two and pry the top one away from the other.

Walt, with his thin sharp edge, was eager to contribute; he turned on his side and tried to get into between the two in the hope of making an entrance.

Porter, as well as Ed seeing this, though he would do likewise and tried to follow Walt's lead. Together they all four pushed and pushed until they had the rocks somewhat separated to the point where now everyone could see that there were indeed two rocks, albeit of different colors.

Both were smooth around the edges once the sides had shifted slightly.

The shifting of the rock gave them something to work. Now all that remained was to lift the top green stone up completely. Dae suggested that by spinning it around clockwise or counter clockwise, they would have four distinct corners for them to work. Despite all of their efforts to lift the top rock, it appeared to be in vain. The momentum they had gathered by shifting the stones to where they had exposed the bottom rock ended.

After everyone's trying and trying for several minutes, they could not get the green one to move any farther, let alone raise it as they were trying to do.

"I say we take a break for a sec," said Loepanda.

"Yes, I agree," said Porter, and the others joined him in agreeing that they should leave it there for a bit and that a break was in order. A break would allow them to catch their breath and regained some strength and try again in a few minutes.

"You know, right about now, some water would be nice and helpful," said Porter laughing, but he was the only one doing so this time.

Brin decided not to take a break and to go on top of the rock to clean the top of it. Perhaps removing the little bit of dirt remaining on the top would somehow make it lighter. Everyone else just sat on the banks watching. They were sitting so far away that they could not see the entire top of it, whereas Brin had a bird's eye view.

Brin, after clearing the top of the green rock could see an inscription.

Although it was in tiny print, that could only see up close; the writing Brin could make out said, 'NOWHERE.'

The others were sitting there on the bank of the hole they had just dug, most of them lay on their backs while others sat upright, just not saying anything to anyone and not even looking at Brin and what he was doing.

Not a moment too soon, the silence was broken when Stan got up and said, "let's get off break, guys, and let's get this done, so we can get on with the rest of our day, let's go about finding the water."

Without comment, they just looked at Stan who was neither the cheerleader for the group or the most enthusiastic about work. His saying everyone should get back to work was a surprise to everyone, and they all silently agreed. No one wanted to appear as if he were less enthusiastic to work than Stan, so slowly but surely, they all got up and stretched their arms to get back to work.

"See how tired we were just a few moments ago, we will need some water, so we can lubricate our mouths and carry on with the show. Going about our day, without water and a break is not the very best way our bodies can take," said Aqualyn.

"Are you sure we can, or should I say, will find water under this thing?" asked Swordan. "Because these stones we have come across here are a lot heavier than I anticipated.' The scorpion was silent.

"What if we were to leave this area and try to find water in another location? Perhaps we will not have to move any large rocks to get to it," said Walt.

"But that would mean we would have to go through the trouble of finding another spot and digging another hole somewhere else, and we know how long it took us to find this spot," said Dae. "And besides, I am very curious to see what is beyond these," Dae continued.

"Without water and a break, it is not the very best way."

"We are already here. Let's finish this," said Ed.

"I agree," said Loepanda. "It could take a while to find water somewhere else, and my sensors tell me that water is not anywhere else out there but generally in this one concentrated spot."

"Ok man that is cool said Porter, but I want to make sure that your sensors sensed water and not stone. I want to make sure your sensors are not all dried up and confused," Porter said, as he continued laughing to himself, as he had done so many times before.

Stan then sprang into action. He was either on a mission to make right on his word or a challenge to get everyone back to work, tapping the underside of the top rock to try and shift it to rise off the other. By this point, for some strange reason, the tools all seemed to be getting their second wind; perhaps it was the fact that Stan somehow took the initiative to get them going, and no one wanted to be upstaged by Stan. No one was quite sure.

The top rock was raised slightly enough by Stan's hitting it underneath. Pebble called over a few of his relatives, and they jumped between the high stone and the bottom one to try to keep it elevated somehow, and then everyone got on it and began to pry it upright.

While everyone preyed the rock upright, Kati got under it and held it in place while Pebble and Ed got at Kati's feet to act as an anchor and keep that in place and prevent Kati from sliding. After struggling for a bit to raise it, they finally got it, but it took all of them, some standing on top of each other.

Once the green rock was removed and stood upright, the underside of it, the part that was on top of the other rock, was now resting on the banks of the sands where everyone could now see its head. Brin had suggested this, so they could see the writing on it.

A lot of sand fell onto the top of the black rock, the one underneath, from all the struggling they had in getting this first rock upright.

Kati held the rock up in place by leaning his body up against it with his arms folded he did not appear to be weak or tired. Brin thought that cleaning the top of the first rock somehow made it lighter and decided to do the same thing to the bottom black one. The others looked at the inscription on the green rock while Brin noticed the black one on the bottom had some engraving on it as well.

Because the tools removed the first without noticing the "NOWHERE" on top of it, they also did not look to see if there was any writing on the other side, which was now covered and resting on the banks. Brin pulled out a few of his strings, tied them around the rock, and everyone gathered and helped pulled it upright. They were all mesmerized and confused as to the meaning of the writing on the first rock, though all it said was "NOWHERE."

Even though Brin had seen the writing of the green first, he had a bad habit of dismissing things as something everyone will find eventually, so he saw no need to alarm or notify the others. Brin again noticed that on the opposite side of the green rock leaning up against the banks was some other writing. This writing appears to be instructions of some sort, but again Brin dismissed it off as a non-issue.

It was too late for them to do anything if needed about the first rock since no one had questioned or investigated what 'NOWHERE' may have meant.

By now it was way too late, even if they realized that they had to take caution or be careful.

Once Brin cleared the top of the second rock, the black one read, "Once the top rock removed; this rock had to be turned over and read and comply with what's written on the other side. Before you proceed, this had to be," it said.

They paused, knowing that somehow, they missed what may or may not have been valuable information or instructions that could benefit, harm or help them somehow. So now they took note as Dae said, "Stop. Let's look at the belly of this green one and see what it said."

The tools leaned the green rock back down slightly away from direct sunlight to read what it said. But all it did was warn about the danger of removing the top rock and not completing the task of the second. Brin took the leadership step of cleaning off the top of the second one, just to see what the instructions on it said.

The tools gathered whatever strength they had remaining and got the first rock entirely out of the way and up on top of the banks and out of the hole.

They began work on the second to try to get it raised and out of the hole and onto the banks as well. They accomplished this the same way they got the first out of the way, by utilizing Kati for a lot of the work.

Brin though he should say something because it just might be important this time since the others missed the other writing on the first. "Guys, I think we should indeed take a look at the writings on this thing," said Brin, referring to the writing on the second stone.

"Well that one here says "NOWHERE,'" said Porter, referring to the top of the first stone that was now out of the way.

Looking at the second rock, they could now clearly see it had some writings of some sort on both sides of it. In addition to the warning of not following the instructions, the top side of the second also said that these rocks got some proper burial.

A proper burial for a set of rocks, I think for this writing it is us it mocks.

These rocks were already beneath the ground, for so many many years, without making a sound.

Then we came along, and it's suddenly our job, our free time it steals, our patience it robs. Well let's see what it all entails, and we go from there, moving faster than a snail," said Aqualyn.

That proper burial included turning them over and placing the green rock on the bottom and then the black rock on the top. If this not done, all the evil in the world would unleash on the planet.

The world would end with a fire that would last a lot longer than the rain. Unlike the storm, which the tools built the giant carrier for, there was nothing in this world they could construct, or they would need to create that could protect themselves, their family, and livestock this time around, from this fire that would destroy everything in its path so nothing would be left to see.

The black rock was held upright by Kati, Swordan, Ed, and Porter so they could see both sides by going around it if needed.

They read and try to understand the top first before going on to try and figure out what the other side of it may say. The writing on the belly was lengthy and very detailed; it appeared to be instructions of some sort. A part of it stated that they had 40 days and 40 nights in which to complete the tasks. They included, among other things flipping the rock upside down and burying it back so that no one could remove it ever again.

No sooner were they getting used to everyone getting along and not missing their homes than they were now back to their old ways again. The finger-pointing began, as each tool blamed the other for losing the writing on the blocks and removing these rocks in the first place. Brin stood in silence fully aware that he was partly to blame for not warning the others about what he had seen firsthand perhaps he could identify where the blame should start or be directed to, since they all had agreed to remove the rock, and they all had worked frantically to get it done.

Porter suggested that Loepanda was to blame, but Roybe said, "no, all Loepanda did was told us where the water was, and no one could blame Aqualyn either because all he wanted was water that they all agreed to help find by digging."

No one was to argue with Dae. After all, he did suggest that they should join and dig a hole for Aqualyn so they could get the water he needed, and so the finger pointing went on.

It was one of those arguments where everyone in the end just had to laugh knowing that you were helpless and no one could do anything about a situation after the fact.

Porter, Ed, and Brin all laughed, knowing they were helpless.

After arguing and blaming each other for not reading the instructions before uncovering the rocks, Swordan yelled, "Quiet, quiet, everyone. If we are going to do this correctly, we are going to have to work together. We have seen in the past how working together actually worked to resolve conflicts and issues that were facing our ancestors before, so we are just going to have to do it again and carry on with what we have to do."

"Look, we could do this in one or two ways," said Dae. We could stand here and argue all day, and nothing will get done, or we could do this as this thing said and finished the job we started.

Dae then raised his hands and asked, "Now all those in favor of finishing what we started, please raise your hands." Everyone raised their hands.

The decision was they would proceed with the project and do as the instructions said.

"Let me look at that rock, and let me read the instructions clearly," said Dae, as he walked up to the rocks and began to read the lengthy instructions on the opposite side. He read some to himself and some out loud, and it included the following:

"As far as they had dug, and all the trouble they have been through to get to this point, all they had to do now was to dig a little deeper, and they would find water," Dae read aloud.

Lordy, how much farther do we have to dig to find this water?" asked Porter, "I would hate to think we would have to dig a lot farther before we find water," he continued.

"Listen up, everyone," said Dae. "There is more. Once we hit the water, we would have to dig one more hole, so we can mix some of the water and sand to create some stone in the same shape as the black and green rock that we would need to complete a project. You can use me to mix the sand and water and shape them into blocks and use these blocks to build the project, the burial ground for these rocks. We need to get everyone together and come up with a plan and figure out a way to execute this plan to solve this issue," said Dae.

Loepanda then said to the group, "Well, folks, our mission is simple, "We need to seal this spot so that all the evil in the world cannot be released and the world come to a fiery end. We will have to dig a little deeper, so we can reach the water."

"First things first. Let's find and get the water out of here. Let's get Aqualyn filled up so it can have all the water it needs, and then we can proceed from there." said Dae.

Dae told Pebble to gather up the rest of his relatives now including the rocks they used to make the fire with last night because they were going to need all the help they could get for this project.

Dae did not read all of it aloud; just the parts he thought were relevant to the others. The instructions were very detailed and precise in its exact specification, and just like the instructions the old man got for the rainy-day project, these instructions were not to be ignored, these steps were not to be skipped. The entire project had to be completed in the time frame specified, and no part of this altered.

The instructions on the rock did contain a detailed diagram and description of what was to be done, just as the one the old man got for the rainy-day project. The instructions included that they were to lay down one layer of rocks that needed to be extended out a little over a specified area. The instructions did specify how large these rocks had to be. To avoid any future conflicts, they got everyone's agreement, and Dae made a point of getting everyone to agree on everything before they proceeded.

Once the first layer was laid down, a second layer had to be laid down directly on top of it, going about six inches inside on top of the first layer.

This was to be continued creating multiple layers of flooring space for this burial project.

The instructions also said before this project was to begin, all of those who discovered this hole were to stand in a circle with one person facing the back of the person in front of him. They were to stand there with their hands on the shoulder of the person in front of them, and they were to remain there until the sun went down.

As the sun went down, they were to keep an eye on their shadows, until the sunset over the dunes.

Wherever their shadows stretched out beyond their heads at the time of sunset, that is how far out the first set of rocks was to be placed at its base.

Then they had to multiply how many of them there were in their group, by the number they got from measuring their shadows. There were eleven of them.

Their shadows stretched out 48 inches beyond their heads. These layers would be one on top of the other.

After laying layer upon layer, and using all the blocks they made, they knew this would take them up to about 480 feet high, give or take. So they had to make sure that they made and used the right size blocks to get this calculation down correctly. They were to take the numbers then they got from the measuring of their shadow, with the number of people in their group and those numbers were the numbers they had to use to build the blocks. Therefore, each block had to be four by eight by eleven. Dae calculated that with that height and base it would take about 2.5 million bricks to complete, and in this case, it was slightly more than eleven acres across.

This was a massive construction project and, unlike the rainy-day project, this was repeated three times. One was to represent the past, the one to the south, the other in the middle, the present, and the third facing the north, the future and each to bury all the evils of those time periods.

The instructions also stated that the edges of the bases needed to point into true north, south, east, and west direction.

Figuring out which section was north, south, east or west was easy. The tools knew that the sun always sets in the west, and it came up in the opposite side, which is the east side, so with that in mind, they knew that if they were to face the sunset, to their left would be the south and to their right was the north. That was their conclusion.

The tools figured that if they took the number of acres and divided it by the number of days needed to complete the project, they would know how fast they had to work. What they had to have done on a day to day basis, so they could finish in time, and it would keep them on schedule.

The tools were not entirely sure as to how to explain the apparent coincidence of the time frame and as to how all the tools came into play. It was too bizarre for them to comprehend, and it was something even Dae did not attempt or could not explain.

They knew a second hole dug up much farther away from where the waterhole was so they could have two holes, one for water and the other to mix the water and sand to make stones or, as they called them, cement blocks to build their project.

The digging of the hole to find the water went on, while Dae continued to read the lengthy instructions. The sand they were picking up was getting moist, and it got damper with every bit of it removed.

Brin was at the bottom brushing away the sand when he suddenly yelled out, "wow, it is wet."

No one thought he was crying wolf; they were more into listening to Dae's reading of the instructions than actually paying any attention to anyone else, including Brin.

Aqualyn did pay attention; he quickly ran down into the hole, saw it was water beyond the wet soil, and got himself filled up. This hole where the water was discovered was the hole they had to cover back up according to the instructions.

Of the three exact structures they had to build, the middle one had to be placed on top of this waterhole, and the other two on either side of it. Once Aqualyn was filled with the water taken from this hole it would have a water supply that would last for over one hundred years, no matter how much of it used. It was a never-ending supply, enough to build the rocks they wanted and enough for Aqualyn to fill up, even long after they covered up this hole, so said the instructions.

The tools knew that the instructions said that whoever discovered this waterhole had to be the ones to complete this project. It was not to be left alone for anyone else to come over and finish. With that, it also meant that all of the tools had to participate in the building of this project; they could not single anyone out and or say, "Well, I did not help to dig or uncover the hole, or it was not my idea to remove the rock.

The very bottom of the instructions stated that this is where all the water went from the rainy-day project that lasted 40 days and 40 nights. This is where that water ended up, and this was the gateway to that reservoir.

What remained a mystery to the tools once they made that discovery was where did all the animals and plant life end up as well? No one knew for sure. They just assumed that, like the water, they were buried somewhere under here, perhaps hidden by the wind shifting the sand around and it was a matter of time, or perhaps never would they ever be located.

But then Dae suggested that all the things and people that did not make it onto the rainy-day project, this is where they buried as well, and these three massive projects were going to keep them hidden forever and prevent them from ever resurfacing by erosions and or natural disasters.

Although it not stated, Dae's suggestion made sense, so they accepted it.

They formed a chain and cleared a path to create a little pond to mix the sand and water to create the cement blocks they needed. They did this by using the same instructions they followed from digging the hole initially when they were digging to look for the water. They then placed some rocks on the ground and then added a few more rocks on the inside of it to build a container and form a seal to pour sand into it and then add water to construct the blocks. The sand used was from the banks and mixed with the water that Aqualyn kept flowing into the second hole they dug up.

Brin's primary function was to brush the sand into the hole. Dae helped as well in transporting the sand that Porter used to mix the sand and water.

Walt, not wanting to feel left out, was asked to use his long pointed bit and turn around in a rapid motion so they could mix the sand and water and perhaps Dae and Swordan could carve out the rocks they needed.

If there were stones, etc., mixed into the sand that needed to be trimmed down into smaller pieces, Roybe, as well as Stan, would then step in and break down those small stones into smaller pieces, bringing them into sand-like form.

The pace was a little slow at first, but then once everyone got their instructions as to what they had to do, they were off and running, and no more second-guessing. The process of making the blocks was started.

As each block was completed, it took just seconds to dry. In fact, from the time the blocks were finished to the time it took them to get the resting place they were dry.

Everyone had a part in this project, and they worked frantically, realizing that this project would take some time, and, unlike the rainy-day project, which took a long time, time is something they did not have a lot of in completing this daunting task.

Again, here they worked in teams, two tools per team. As one tool got tired, they would switch places with the other and continue working.

Despite the fact that earlier everyone was bickering about removing these rocks without first reading the instructions, all of that bickering and bitterness and evil comments were now all gone. The tools came to realize that for them to survive together, it meant they had to work together, and the plan set forth for everyone seemed to work for everyone's liking at this point. The architectural engineering involved in building this was more than they at first imagined.

With everyone going about their specified way working on this project, Loepanda soon realized that he was the only one standing around not doing anything to contribute to its completion. He could not even offer words of comfort or encouragement to the tools. At this point, they were more caught up in their work than ever before. He decided the best thing for him to do since it appeared to him that his job here done, was to leave, but in doing so, he would have to bid the tools farewell and good luck first. Not wanting to interrupt their work schedule or their pace, Loepanda just walked around to each tool and shook hands to say goodbye. He wished them all the best of luck and continued success for the remainder of their time. He expressed his joy in knowing he was essential in helping them locate the water for their projects, as well as water to recharge themselves and helping to explain where all that water from the rainy-day storm of several lifetimes ended up.

It was not as if they ignored Loepanda, but the tools were so focused on this project, that a simple goodbye to Loepanda was all they could afford. This frantic pace continued for days and days on end, with the tools working for more than 12 hours a day at times. They stopped only for a limited time to get a drink of water or so.

It was almost surreal that during the first two projects and the first two days they were here, no one wanted food or water that badly, and now that they had water that would last forever, they were now thirsty.

Stan came into this not knowing what he had to do, or what he could do.

He had feared he was over and done with and about to retire, but now he and Walt were very excited to play a part.

One of Stan's functions was to knock the blocks into place by tapping them on edge, and Brin just cleared away the rough edges around the outside of the rocks, so any excess cement would not hang over the sides. Swordan captured most of the excess cement that Brin brushed off and took it back to remixed into the other cement. This excess cement, though, once it fell off, it did not dry in seconds as the blocks did. It was as if it was waiting, knowing it would be used again and again.

There is an old saying that "time flies when you are doing new things," and this was the situation in which Pebble now found himself. He was having so much fun he did not realize that the time had also come for him to move on.

Pebble had long since determined that his work here finish, but he was enjoying the company of the tools particularly that of Stan. Now he felt useless and perhaps he was just in the way of everyone. Since no one wanted to stop working, especially to chit chat with him, he thought the best thing to do was just to leave. He stood on the bank, cleared his throat, and clapped his hands three times in about three seconds, one clap per second to get everyone's attention, and he did, briefly.

"To be a hero of tomorrow, we have to be super today. To build a solid foundation for the future, we must build on the groundwork of the past," said Pebble as he began to walk forward to shake the hands of all the tools.

Everyone, this time, did stop working but it was only for a brief moment, long enough to listen to Pebble's departing words.

They one by one they all shook his hands and wished him well in his travels, but soon after their goodbye, it was back to work for them as Pebble moved onto the next person.

He bid them all a final farewell, as he walked off waving his hand in the air.

As Pebble walked away, he said, "When you all return to your world, you will miss all this nice heat with abundant sunshine."

"So long my friend, and best of luck to you," said Porter, but not before making one last parting shot to Pebble, a function only Loepanda did before.

"So, what do you call a rock that propels high above all the other rocks in everything he does?" asked Porter.

"That's an easy one," yelled back Pebble. "You call him a rocket."

The two laughed and waved to each other and Pebble continued on his way.

No one even noticed when Pebble disappeared into the distance.

"Oh, no," said Walt. The storm is gone by now, we must have been here for over a year."

It was as if no one heard him. He stopped to make his comment, but everyone just continued working. They had other things on their minds. He assumed that either they did not hear him or were ignoring him.

But the tools continued to build the base of their project, as each plate required another base placed on top of it etc., etc., etc., each layer about 2 feet in from the bottom layer. The sun was blazing, and it seemed at times, the harder they worked, the harder it bore down on them. The sun, they thought, was working in opposition with them, and it was trying to slow them down in some manner. The more sweating they did, the more water Aqualyn had to provide for them.

Aqualyn provided all the water they needed; after all, he had a never-ending supply to go around.

Day after day, and sometimes late into the night, they would work on this project, and as the day turned into the night, they would rest, but only long enough to return to it the first thing in the morning of the next day. The water that Aqualyn provided was more than enough to recharge their batteries in the morning, and it also acted as breakfast, lunch, and dinner for everyone.

Slowly but surely the project began to take shape, and once one it was completed, they knew they had to get going on the other one. There was no time for play or small talk or reflection on one the finished part.

"Remember, guys, we have two more of these things to build," Dae would say.

With one done, they immediately started to work on the next one and then the next, until all three what appeared to be upside down cone-shaped projects were now completed.

It seemed as though the work took about three weeks to complete, even though nobody was paying any attention to the time, and no one kept track of the days. But there was a general sense of satisfaction that they had finished it in record time and it was brilliant and spectacular.

Day number twenty-one, of the third week of the project, was a sad day; all the work was finally complete just before high noon when they placed the last block on top. This last block symbolically was set by Dae, and just before he went up to put it on the head, he held it up high into the air and pointed it towards the sun. He held it in silence, although everyone was on edge, waiting for some words of encouragement, or a 'good job' speech.

They stood in front of the project, not saying a word, although they were proud of the work they had done and the contribution everyone had in it. Side by side, they stood and placed their hands around each other's waists and stared up at the finished project.

There were no tears, or cheers of laughter or jubilee celebration, just a somber recognition that they finished, and perhaps they saved humanity and future generations a lot of problems.

"The greatest test of a man's vision is his ability to lead," said Dae. "The best he can do for his future is not to forget his past. For him to have happiness tomorrow, he must enjoy today."

Everyone was silent and stood to stare at the project, as Dae was speaking.

"For us to correctly map the future, we must first understand the blueprints of the past."

He went on "For us to enjoy the treasures of tomorrow, we must protect those of the past."

"Well done, guys," well done," was all each said to the other, but still no tears or smiles. Dae then placed the last rock on the top.

All of the anger, sadness and hard feelings that were so common at the beginning of this project were now gone. There was nothing but congratulations and warm wishes for everyone. It was as if no one wanted the work to come to an end, they enjoyed each other's company so much, and worked so hard together and grew so close together that it was almost as if a part of them, as one of the tools was leaving. This project now buried all the evil, bad feelings and anger they once felt for each other.

"History will look back in time on these things one day and wonder how these came about, how they built it, why they made it, who created them and how long did it take. They would ask, "how did anyone come up with this idea? Who thought of this? and what were they thinking? Was this what they had in mind?" and a million more questions that will all lead to other issues. Questions about not just this project but also about the rocks to the north of us, Stonehenge, and the rainy-day project as well. Questions future generations will have to ponder for more generations to come.

The answers to which only we, the tools that built these projects, will know the answers and the reasons why," said Dae.

"Today we see projects built, projects like giant multi-lane bridges, skyscrapers, and stadiums. We know the reason, the way, the infrastructure involved, and the tools involved in such a project. We also know how long it takes to build them and what the cost is, but they will never measure up to these monuments of the past, these wonders of civilization" Dae continued.

There was silence, then, "Well, gentlemen, my work here is done, I must leave in the direction of the sun," said Aqualyn, "and I must move on. It has been like heaven while we worked through hell, leaving your mark on history for future generations to tell."

"I congratulate you on the fine job you have done. This will be admired by generations to come, but I must go now, I have to continue on my way, but I will look forward to the future and another day," he continued. "I am not sure where it will lead me to, and what I will encounter and what I will do. Who I will meet along the way, and how

I will miss you guys and what we have done this day, but when I get to where I am going, I know in my heart that I am full of pride, and it will be showing."

"I will always remember these projects, I will walk past them with care, and every time I come by this way, it is upon them that I will stare. I will also head up north to visit the rock; I will always remember the lessons we learned from the school of hard knocks.

I will share my stories of you with them, the way we were together, our hard feelings would mend, and of the great adventures we had in building these projects that will last forever and ever like the seas," Aqualyn continued.

With that Aqualyn waved goodbye to all the tools, but unlike the others, Aqualyn did not go to each tool and bid them farewell, he just turned to everyone and waved to them all, and off he went about his way.

"Well, gentlemen, let's get on home, we are finished, let's go home now," said Swordan.

Lordy, thank goodness we are going home," said Porter. "I could not go on another day out here. I will be happy to be home so that I can recharge fully. I need a vacation."

"I think I will go to one of those Caribbean islands that continuously have hurricanes passing through; I could be boarding up doors and windows forever, he continued.

THE JOURNEY HOME

"Okay let's go," as Brin and Kati took off leading the way, brushing the part where they would have to walk back to the shed. And off they all went heading back towards the shed no one looking back on the barren desert behind them, or the projects they just had completed. They were not even thinking of the hole they had dug up to find the water and mix the blocks, or of the vultures, they feared would come down and get them. All of that was now behind them. No one looked back wondering "what if," or "if only."

The journey back into the shed took them one whole day to complete, and they did not rest anywhere along the way. It was as though they found their second wind again, or the last bit of water they drank was energy water to fuel them back to the shed. Whatever it was, something was giving them the fuel they needed to complete the trip again. Everyone seemed to be in a hurry to get back into the shed, although no one could say the particular reason why.

They had grown and accomplished so much together, now as well as their ancestors, so it was somewhat of a mystery to everyone why they had these feelings of wanting to leave. Perhaps it was the fear of running into another visitor or discovering they had to do something else, something Dae forgot to mention that was part of the instructions on the rocks before they got home, but whatever the reason was, they wanted to leave.

No one, not even Dae, could explain why it took only one day to get back to the shed, but so many to get to where they were, and no one cared either. Along the way back, the topic of conversation once again became the projects they had just built. The questions arose, including what they would have done differently if they had to do it over again, and what they wish they could build together, knowing what is involved in getting things like that made.

Although no one had any regrets about what they had done, Walt and Roybe, while walking and talking to each other, brought up the conversation and mentioned that they wish they could have built a bridge over the rivers, and widened the streams as well.

"Anyone have anything else they would like to add to this?" asked Walt.

"The one thing I would like to have done was to build a garden where they could grow some food and flowers to make the place look better. But above all others, I am happy with the one thing we did build, that was our friendship," said Dae.

The pace picked up considerably as the shed was now in view, and although it was hot, they went from a quiet stroll to a brisk walk, to a run. Now the shed was a few feet away. When they reentered the shed, it was just as they left it before, nothing had moved, and the master Joseph had not even entered it once. This was unusual they thought because coming into the shed was something he did almost every day, sometimes even several times a day. Also, if he did enter the shed, he must not have noticed anything missing from it, or he must not have needed anything in it at that time.

As the tools returned to the shed, they stood on the floor where they first met each other, and there was silence. No one wanted to be the first to utter the words "goodbye." Although they were eager to leave the desert, it was not something they hoped to be doing anytime soon. It was an uncomfortable and contrasting happy and at the same time a sad situation.

Kati, who had not said much of anything through the trip, surprised everyone with being the first to speak. He kept it brief and just said, "So long," as he walked back over and into the corner where he was leaning and just folded his arms. What emotion he was going through no one will ever know, because he did it so quickly and faced the wall as he disappeared into the dark corner blending in with the color.

It was clear to everyone that Swordan and Kati were not very good at farewells. This was something new to them except for saying goodbye to Aqualyn and Pebble. They had not had the experience of having a new tool come into their midst for as long as they could remember, and whatever new tool came to join them, that tool never left.

Swordan just waved, and they began to place themselves in the place where their home was. They all knew they were about to go on and leave the memories behind them, the memories that they had made all this time.

Those memories left behind also left no one with happy faces. Everyone realized that they were about to go, and perhaps never see each other again. Maybe they would meet again via a distant relative in a movie, book or a museum, but for right now the uncertainty was sad for them.

Although only knowing each other for a brief moment, the tools knew that each would remain in the others' minds for a long, long time. Now all that remained in the middle of the floor were the tools from the new world, as the old tools looked on anxiously to see how they would leave or where they would go to get home.

No one even heard from Arial. All that was left was the writing of the words, "so long" on the ground in front of them, and then he vanished.

It was quiet then a brisk wind came through the shed. The tools stood in the foreground with a stone-faced look. The wind brought in a smell that no one could recall smelling before.

"It smells like feet," said Porter. No one else commented.

"Now when I count to three, I want you all to close your eyes and keep them closed until I tell you to open them. Open them when I again count to three and say openly" said Dae.

All the tools closed their eyes before Dae began to count and waited for Dae's instructions. As Dae counted to three the first time, he paused for about ten seconds, not saying a word, while the tools just stood there with their eyes closed, and Swordan looked on. Then just as he was about to begin to count to three for a second time the wind again came through the shed, but this time with it came a dust cloud that encompassed all the tools and blinded Swordan briefly. It had a more pleasant smell. They could not see each other for a few seconds that seemed to last forever.

"One, two, three," said Dae.

The cloud passed, they all opened their eyes, and they were back inside the garage.

"Wow." was all Swordan could say, as he, Kati and Arial were once again alone.

Realizing they were back in their home, inside the garage, they looked around, and nothing had changed from when they left. They were back in the garage and on the counter, but this time the rain had stopped, and they could see beams of sunlight coming from the cracks in the garage telling them that it was bright and sunny outside.

Porter ran over and looked out the window and shouted, "Wow, I can see traffic and skyscrapers. Yes, we are home, yes, we are home," he said yelling with his fist in the air and jumping up and down.

Sitting still in awe of the whole experience, Dae said to Porter and Walt, "You guys are new, you are the builders of the future, and we are the builders of the past. One day, whether we like it or not, there will be newer and more skilled tools introduced into the marketplace that I am afraid, will make all of us all one day obsolete. When that day comes, I want you to look back on the past, know where you came from, what you have accomplished, what your ancestors helped to create, and look back on your life without any regrets, or disappointment."

Looking around the garage, they could see that it was now early morning, and on this morning, as they had not seen in the previous mornings, the sun came up, but this time there was some morning fog outside. You could look at the sunbeams coming through the mist in the distance. For the first time in what seemed to be an eternity, they heard the roosters outside waking up to a brand-new day. It was a sound they had missed and a sound they were glad to hear again, although when they were here, and it would sound off every morning, they had somehow managed to mute the sound of the rooster.

But then there was another sound, one which they were very familiar with, and one which they also had not heard in quite some time either.

It was the sound of the garage door opening up. This startled all the tools.

"Yes, is it morning already," said Walt.

Sam, the house owner, walked in and stood in the doorway looking at his tools in the garage. He clapped his hands once while rubbing them together and said out loud, "Well, well, what a beautiful day ahead of me."

He walked over to his rolling cart, grabbed it and rolled it over to the counter and began to place some tools on the wagon. He grabbed Roybe, Walt, and Porter, and put them on the rolling cart first.

He paused and looked at the other tools, then turned around and rolled it out of the garage.

The other tools, the shovel, and all the screwdrivers looked at the tools on the rolling cart as it was being rolled away and winked at them. The tools gave them a thumbs up and said, "Go get 'em guys," and "remember never do a good job, do a great one," said Dae.

Sam then walked out with the rolling cart in hand to where he was about to start building his deck. Smiling and whistling along the way, the tools knew what job they had ahead of them. After all, Sam had mentioned, today was the day he was going to build his deck.

As he pulled the cart out and stood outside, he already had a backhoe clearing the path where he was going to build his deck.

This bright yellow backhoe, almost one thousand times the size of any of the tools in the garage, but by no means the same age as any of them. It seemed much younger than even Porter, but no way as old as Dae. He looked at the small tools coming out of the garage on the rolling cart and said out loud to them, "Wow you guys are small."

His deep trembling voice was enough to frighten the tools, who looked up at this monster of a device and wondered how he came about to be able to dig up such a large hole and clear this much space in such a small amount of time and doing it all by himself.

They thought Sam must have been out here early in the morning to get all of this done.

Walt turned to Roybe and said, "This is it, this is what Dae was talking about, these are the new and improved tools that will replace us in the future, it is already happening."

"Yes, the days of men using us to do all this hard work is over. "We are obsolete," said Roybe.

The backhoe dug a hole where a shovel once did that work. He cleared away all the trees and brush in the yard in no time flat, a job the rocks once did for the rainy-day project.

The garden, now cleared, looked like the area they had just come from, except the dirt was more fertile. It reminded them of the ground where the large carrier landed and how perfect it was. You could see specks of the moist grass here and there.

"If that thing digs any deeper, it will find water," said Porter.

Sam picked up the wood he was going to use for the base and began to place it on the treated ground side by side as in a hardwood floor installation formation.

After the first layer of wood was down, he then picked up another set and began to place them in the opposite direction on top of the ones that laid down before.

These pieces of wood had indentations which allowed them to interlock into each other along the way.

"Wow," said Porter. "It is like building the pyramids all over again."

"I wonder if this project would stand up to the test of time, the kind of test the wood from the rainy-day project had to endure," asked Roybe.

"We will sure find out one day, won't we, we will surely find out," said Porter.

The tools wondered if he was trying to copy or do a similar formation to the pyramids or if all construction is done this way.

"Well, perhaps Sam is trying to bury something down here. Perhaps it is memories he would rather not have around, yes, the memories of all the nagging from his wife, or perhaps he, too, was hearing voices that told him he needed to do this," said Ed, looking at the garage.

After placing the wood pieces on top of each other to make his base, Sam reached and grabbed Porter and started to shoot the nails into the wood. It was not the same feeling Porter had building the blocks project; there was no sense of belonging, he just wanted to get this job done and over. The deck base slowly began to take shape, and it was very reminiscent of the pyramid they had just completed, but without the enthusiasm, they felt.

Next, he placed poles, standing them upright on the outside, which could support the roof and the sides of the deck. The poles standing upright reminded the tools of Stones over the hedge, and the roof of the shed that was already built and lying down on the ground across the way reminded them of the rainy-day project.

The roof was already built, and it was purchased from the hardware store as one complete piece and meant only to cover part of the deck; about half of it was to remain exposed. This was a pity for Sam, the tools thought. Joseph built all of his baby carriers from the ground up, using all raw materials and they thought Joseph was a far better carpenter than Sam was or would ever be.

The roof was also to have hooks so Sam's wife could hang some flowers and plants around on the outside of it. These were the only flowers and plants she planned to keep. They were all that remained of her once proud garden. Sam's wife now wanted cactus plants and other low maintenance plants around her house; she was no longer into roses and the vegetables she once craved.

Dae watching from a distance, could not help but comment, "The more things change, the more we go back to the past and redo or try to bring back what was done before."

After the sides were up, Sam used Roybe to cut off the excess wood from not only the top, but also from the base of his deck, and then he got a vacuum to get rid of the excess dust, a job Brin once did.

Brin was by no means saddened by seeing this. He was quite happy not to be involved in this particular project. He considered this project minute compared to what he had just accomplished, and finding all the things his family had discovered, like the dinosaurs, he thought this job beneath him.

"This should not sadden you, that's the way society is; it is the price we pay for progress," said Roybe after staring at Brin. Staring at the vacuum doing the job he once did, Brin responded, "Not that it saddens me, in fact, I am quite happy."

People today want to make things easier and more comfortable, and they want to do more with less effort. As we rely more and more on the powerful and smaller tools to do our work for us, in doing so we tend to be less active, and thus we encounter more health problems later on in life," said Dae. "That's the problem with society in general, we want results now, and we want it easier, and we want the answers now. Technology, if not used and implemented correctly, will be the end of us all," Dae continued.

Sam, proud of the job he had done, placed the tools down, and stood in the middle of his deck, with his hands on his hips, and looked around at his new deck. He then walked over to the backhoe he was using to clear the place, and sat in the seat of the backhoe, turned on the key and the engine again rumbled. The thundering sound of the backhoe and the smoke coming out of the bellows, made the tools wonder what Sam was up to now. They were used to the compressor that Porter usually had to connect to and the noise it made whenever it was turned on, but this was different.

"That cannot possibly be healthy," said Roybe, "It appears as though this new tool is ill," he continued. But the backhoe did not make any comments back.

Sam began to reverse it out of his driveway into the road and then onto an awaiting truck that was going to transport it back to the home improvement store where he had rented it from for the weekend. The tools just looked at the backhoe, rolling down the driveway.

"Wow, not only does this tool do all the work for itself, but instead of the owner carrying this tool around, this tool carries the owner. That is a sign of progress, and something we have never seen before," said Ed, looking out at the tools.

As the backhoe was rolled onto the truck to transport back, it never said a word; it never waved, never made any parting gestures, movement or anything, like it did when it first saw them. It was as if he was unaware or did not care to meet and greet any of the tools. He seemed as though he just wanted to leave.

"You see, even he is not satisfied with the job he has just done," said Brin, laughing.

But on its way out, it did look back a few times, even though it did not make any comment or gestures to the tools or at the deck now completed. Perhaps it wanted to see one last time the finished work, or maybe he wanted to look at the tools he had just replaced.

With the backhoe now back on the truck, Sam quickly ran back inside the house, leaving the tools outside on the rolling cart to get his wife. He invited his wife out to stand on the deck and walk around it.

Sam walked out with his wife. He had her cover her eyes with a blindfold so she could not see the finished project until she was standing on top of it. The tools just sat there in the corner on the cart.

With Sam's wife standing directly in the middle of the deck, he slowly removed the blindfold, so she could see the finished project.

She smiled and said to him, "Honey I am so proud of you," as she stood there with her hands over her mouth. "With the right tools, you can do anything. This is very, very nice," she continued.

An overjoyed Sam then picked her up and spun her around several times in the air, as she laughed out loud, holding him as she swirled around.

"That is what it is all about," said Dae, "building something that someone will enjoy for quite some time, which is the reward of our job."

Sam took the cart and started rolling the tools back into the garage. The tools thought he would put them back into their place. Sam's wife did as she promised and no longer complained about all the tools he had all over the place now that she had her deck and he promised to get rid of the old tools he was cultivating.

Sam was so excited about his new deck and he seemed to be in such a hurry that he quickly closed the garage door, turned the lights out and left.

Sam slammed the door on his way out and left the tools on the cart. They were quiet for a while.

"Well that's it, another job is well done. This time, I wonder, what was the satisfaction we got out of building this project we just completed," said Walt.

"There will be no pat on the back, no job well done, and no one I know or no one I will get to know will be able to enjoy this for generations to come. As soon as this house sold, if it sold, the new owners will want to remodel it and perhaps get rid of the deck, and put in a garden," said Walt.

"Perhaps new tools will be used to remove the deck or replace it with whatever they have to replace it with in the future."

It was a sad, quiet couple of moments for the tools with no one feeling appreciated for what they had just accomplished. It was like doing a great job and having your supervisor or another employee take all the credit. There was no sense of accomplishment, no feel-good feeling, even though some of the tools worked together on this one.

Before the tools could say much of anything or reflect on what they had just done, the silence was interrupted by a scratching sound coming from the floor. As the tools looked down, they saw a centipede crawling across the floor of the garage.

"Where did he come from?" Brin asked out loud.

The centipede stopped and looked up and asked, "Where did I come? You talking to me, you can't be talking to me."

This little guy was about nine inches long and an inch and a half including his legs at its widest point. He had a black top and a light gold looking trim along the side. He spoke as if he had something in his mouth, or his tongue was tied in some way.

Although he spoke without a stutter, you could hear there was some effort in his speech.

"I tell you from where I came. I bury beneath all that grass and dirt that your owner just dug up to build his deck. That was my home, now it has been foreclosed on, so I had to move," he said in an angry tone and slamming his hands on the floor.

He told the tools this while yelling and pointing his hands at not just the tools, but in every direction and using a very aggressive voice. The tools looked at each other, not saying a word, as the centipede continued.

"One day I am sitting in my house, a big house with lots of leg room, next thing I know, I am homeless, I lose everything, not a leg to stand on. I tell you there is no respect," he continued.

"You know who you remind me of, Loepanda," said Walt. All the tools looked at him because they had heard Loepanda make similar remarks about getting no respect, something Loepanda picked up from a very famous comedian who has since passed.

Most of the tools' first conclusion was to naturally to assume that the two of them were related in some way. But they just listened as the centipede continued.

"I had to get out of that house anyway," continued the centipede, "There was not enough room to store my shoes. I felt like a supermodel downsizing."

He said this laughing, but no one laughed with him. No one got the joke. It was because no one knew any supermodels.

"This guy walks in, one minute he is all angry, now he is all laughing," said Brin.

Just like Loepanda telling jokes about Pebble, the centipede got no immediate response from the tools, but he kept on saying his jokes.

"Driving a car for me is not easy either. I have to have one set of legs on the brakes and one set on the gas, all I do is rev the engine."

Again no one responded with laughter.

"When I was a baby, I took baby steps." He laughs out loud. "Get it, baby steps," he continued, holding his stomach. "When I went for walks with my mom and dad, I had to walk twice as fast to keep up with them; it was a two-step process."

"Get it, twice as fast, two steps." Again no one laughed, that did not stop him from carrying on.

"But seriously, folks, let me tell you a serious story here for a second.

This is the story of my life. This is the story as to how my life has been in the past few years. Listen please."

All the tools nodded their heads saying, Yes, they would listen," even though they have not spoken a word directly to him, or suggested to him that they were not listening.

"I answered this newspaper ad for a house helper one day. The ad said you must know how to, cook, clean, wash, mop, and perform basic house cleaning. I get to the interview, and the interviewer asked me, 'So do you know how to wash, cook, clean, mop, etc.?' I said to him, "Hey, look at me, I have 40 hands. Not only can I do all that, but I can also knit you a sweater while I am doing all of that. When finished, I think I will want to mow the lawn, wash the car, and paint the side of the house while I am at it all at the same time.

The interviewer apparently did like my sarcasm. I think he thought he should be the only one to be funny because he looked at me and asked, 'Yes, but can you also roast marshmallows and make biscuits from scratch?' He laughed when he asked me that.

So I asked him, (So do I have the job or not?) He said, in a serious tone, 'We'll get back to you,' and you know that is code for, don't call us, we will call you, and so I left. He never called," said the centipede as he nodded his head as if he was about to cry.

Although he did not cry, he just nodded his head for the sake of nodding it.

Perhaps it was to get a sympathetic response from the tools or some comment, or it was just his way of saying that this part of his story was over. He raised his head quickly.

"I went to another interview, this one was at a circus, and this is where I thought at first that I had found my calling. The day I got there for my interview, the regular juggler was out sick, so I walked up to the interviewer and introduced myself.

I shook his hands with four of my hands, unusual for me because I usually only use one or two hands and that is if I like you. He told me about the juggler out sick, and so I asked, 'What good is a circus without a juggler?'

The interviewer tells me that with the juggler out sick, they desperately needed someone to fill his shoes, get it, fill his shoes," said the centipede.

"Again no one laughs. He coughs as if to clear his throat and did not appear to be distraught or saddened by the lack of laughter. The centipede continued his story.

When I walked in, however, the place was empty, the stage was empty, the animals were all grumpy, and the show was to go on that evening.

As I sat down with the interviewer, he asked me, 'Do you know how to juggle, can you fill his shoes?' The juggler that was out sick was a spider, I said, "Listen, buddy, this guy has eight legs, I have 40, not only can I fill his shoes, but I will have enough feet left over to fill his gloves as well. And not only can I juggle, but I can also cook, clean, mop, do windows, the dishes, roast marshmallows, mow the lawn, paint the house and make biscuits from scratch, all at the same time."

"He also did not see the humor in that, so I looked at him and said, 'You know, my last interview did not get that either,' continued the centipede."

"So, did you get the job?" asked Porter.

"Well, yes," said the centipede. "Needless to say, I got the job, and that very night was my first night on the job, and I had it all planned perfectly. I had a trick where I laid on my back, and I juggled everything from chainsaws to fireballs, etc." He moved his hands in a motion as if he was juggling something.

"It was great, you guys are going to love this, check this out," said the centipede.

He stood straight on his back twenty legs, ten on each side, with his other twenty legs in the air, moving his hands back and forth as if he was juggling something, to demonstrate how things are manipulated.

"While juggling, I had a sneeze attack, ha, ha, ha," he laughs out loud," and I blew a ball of fire into the air and burst the balloons and caused a panic. I missed the chainsaw as well, and it cut the rope that the acrobats were using to cross over on.

They came falling to the floor, it was hilarious, and he held his stomach again laughing.

The crowd loved it, but my boss did not think it was all that good, not even funny, because he had to repurchase all that equipment, and he was without the trampoline guys for the next performance as well so he had to let me go.

"Wow," said Dae. "Talk about your job of the week."

"Not to despair," said the centipede. The very next day I got another job offer, this one at a car wash, no exceptional skills were needed, and it was comfortable washing cars. I never liked that job from my first day, but I took it because, one, I needed the money and, two, the pay and hours were tenfold, and also because everybody would sit back and watch and learn as I did all the work. I did enjoy being in the spotlight. I would wash the car while at the same time I would dry it while cleaning the tires, vacuuming the inside and waxing it all at the same time. Everyone would stand back and watch me work, it was as if they had nothing better to do, or did not want to do anything, so I had to get out of there.

I felt overwork and underpaid for the amount of work I was doing even though the day was excellent.

"So is that the shortest job you ever had?" Dae asked the centipede. "How long did that job last," Dae continued.

"Oh, man, I was in and out of there in two hours, that job lasted all of two hours," the centipede continued. "I quit and decided to become a nomad and wander from place to place.

I am not sure what I want to do with my life, and in what direction I want to go," said the centipede. "I settled here for a bit, and I have been here for about 40 days now. I was going to make this my home, and now my home is no more."

Dae looked at him and, judging from his mannerism and features, asked him if he knew of his family tree, and if he knew from where he came regarding his ancestors.

"I do not pay any attention to that stuff. My family is made up of me, myself and I. I am my family," he replied.

Dae told him about the scorpion they met. Even though he was not related to the centipede, but like the centipede, it, too, was somewhat disliked and feared and misunderstood by many. He used his natural sense to do a lot of good, and he encouraged the centipede to do likewise.

The centipede thought about it for a bit, scratched his head and wondered what good he could do for society.

"I'll think about it," he said, as he winked at Dae.

"You know what, though," said the centipede. "I guess what I want to say is this. No matter what life throws at you as it did me, you have to pick yourself up and move on, because no matter how good we are or how talented we think we are we can all be replace in the blink of an eye," said the centipede. "That's one of the cruel lessons that life would teach us. No matter what life throws at you, no matter what jobs you go to, just remember, you should never do a good job, always do a great one. Somewhere out there, there is someone who is waiting to do it better, faster, cheaper, and in less time, and they are all wanting to do just that."

After being silent for a moment, he said, "I think I will think about it but what I want to be is a comedian. And with that, he slowly walked away from them, as the scratching sound continued across the floor. Everyone thought perhaps he would say something else or stay a little longer, but he abruptly ended his story and left. There were no goodbyes, no waves, nothing he just went.

Lordy! Okay, talk about your passing act," said Porter.

As the centipede walked away through a hole in the wall, the tools all waved their goodbyes to him.

It was silent again, with nothing to do and nothing to build, nothing on the horizon now that the deck was completed.

"So is anyone for a game of PHZED?" asked Ed. There was a loud resounding "No!" from all the tools.

"Okay, okay, just thought I would ask," said Ed, laughing.

But among all the mumbling, and chatter, Walt wanted to be heard.

He coughed to get everybody's attention. Yes, he had something to say.

"I want to thank you all for helping me see my past and understand my future. The tools of the past do have some relevance in the future, and I thank you all for helping me to see that. There was a loud round of applause as he said, "Thank you all," waving his hands in the air side to side.

Stan then slammed himself down onto the countertop as a judge does in a courtroom to get everyone's attention. It was not that he did not want them to listen to Walt, but Walt finished, and he wanted to be next.

"Well, I was sitting here banging my head against the wall wondering what I was going to say. I am not sure where I would be without any of you. You were all instrumental in helping tools like me and making me feel useful. My cousin is entering a Mr. Sledge universe contest, and he is so big and muscular he has an excellent chance of winning this. I do not think any of us can look back on our lives and say we indeed made it on our own, that we were our tool. We all, at some point, needed the help of someone else to get us where we are, and we will always need each other in some capacity. There are some functions that we as one cannot do at all.

I thank you all, and I love you all." there was a round of applause from everyone.

The feeling they had, in the beginning, had now returned, that feeling of openness and outpouring of emotions and talking about themselves.

Next up was Brin.

Well, we have coughed to get everyone's attention and banged our heads against the wall to do the same thing. Me, I have just swept my way into the audience, and I say to them. Throughout history, great artists have used my people, or so I have been told.

I recall the stories like the one of my cousin who painted the Mona Lisa, and even today my family is still working on these large archeological sites throughout the world, making all those great discoveries.

"I think, for me, the greatest story I heard was of my relatives in the western United States helping to discover the buried dinosaurs and helping to get them all cleaned up and displayed in a museum. That was my greatest reward and inspiration. I look back on that and say, yes, my people did that, and we cleared the part to that discovery."

There was a unanimous agreement to what Brin had to say as well, as they all nodded their heads and said yes.

Roybe was a relatively new tool in this garage and was without a lot of history.

Countries such as the United States and Australia, are wonderful, but their history like mine is that of a concise one.

He said he had heard the numerous stories of the sawmill, and since then they had made him smaller and smaller to fit in more unique places.

"As far as recent history, I can recall the jokes people would make of me since I was so new, jokes like, "What do you call grass that cuts people. Well sawgrass, of course,' and what do you call a fish that cuts someone as opposed to biting them? A sawfish. "Well, let me cut to the chase, or so to speak. I love being here with all of you and I truly look forward to building more in the future, just as we have done so many times in the past."

He also received a round of applause from the other tools.

Well, last but not least up was Dae.

No matter what the topic of conversation among the tools was, whenever Dae spoke, everyone got quiet and listened. From explaining the game to talking about how they are to be used and cared for, whenever Dae spoke, they all had to be silent and stop whatever they were doing. It was as if it was the law.

Dae stood up, looked from one end of the tools lined up to the other with no expression on his face, but a nod, with one hand folded inside the other.

He then placed one hand his right on his chest, and the other crossed over with the elbow resting on it and holding his chin.

He looked up at the tools and said, "From the beginning of man, we have seen and built great things together in the past and will do so in the future. I know the constructions of the past are a mystery to today's society, but we the tools know all too well how they got there because we have heard the stories from our ancestors and their ancestors. Look at the world now. In today's society, we have skyscrapers that continue to defy height. Every time someone builds a great one, someone else comes along and tops it, and we continue to build monuments and symbols that challenge our way of thinking and excite our senses."

"No one knows for sure what tomorrow will bring, what is new and what will improve upon in the future, or what new landmark we will construct.

But be assured that we will all play a part in it as we did in the past, doing better and more significantly than in the past. Individually we may move some dirt, but collectively we can dismantle a mountain. I will rest assured knowing that in all this we will always be a part of each other."

Dae received a standing ovation, as always is the case. All the tools just hugged and patted each other on the backs, as a few of them shed a tear or two. It was the feeling they had when they left the shed, but without the actions that followed.

The screwdriver's kids were off playing a game alone in the corner and did not participate. Their somber celebration and collective pampering were about to end.

The doors opened once again, and a sudden silence fell inside the garage as Sam opened the door and walked in with a bag in his hand. All the tools sat there in silence as he made his way down the side of the garage. He stopped and placed the bag on the counter and looked around the garage at the other tools with his hands still holding onto the bag.

The tools just stared at him as he stood there, staring back at them.

Sam opened the bag and pulled out a brand-new tool and placed it on the counter.

He then pulled out the detachable plug that came with it and plugged it into the tool and the other end into the outlet on the wall. Two red lights began to flash, perhaps indicating that the tool was charging; the other tools looked on, particularly at the light.

Never before have they seen a tool with two flashing lights. This was new to them as well.

The two lights did not flash together. However, they did blink rapidly, and when one was on, the other was off, like a police car. Sam, did not say anything, left it plugged in and walked outside again.

Not wanting to be rude to the new tool, all the old tools walked over slowly towards the new kid on the block and to get a good look at him and to check him out, as they did when they were told to by Dae when they first met Walt and Roybe.

The tools all gathered in front of the new tool to get a closer look. No one said anything as they approached. They just looked on in curiosity as they approached even more intimate and surrounded this new tool.

Recalling what had happened when they first met Walt and Roybe when they were scared of meeting them, they did not want any surprises from this new tool, but they expected at least one.

After what seemed to be a few minutes of them looking at it and its red light still flashing, Walt pointed his bit at the tool and poked it to try and get a response, but there was no response. The tools thought that this new tool was ignoring them or perhaps it was asleep. Maybe that is what the red flashing light meant: Stop or do not disturb.

There was a mixture of emotions as to whether they should let it sleep or whether they try to get some response from it. No one knew for sure.

But then the red light stopped flashing, and it made a single beeping sound when it ended. The red light turned off, and a green one came on.

"You broke it," said Roybe to Walt.

There was still no response from the new tool, only the change in light.

The door reopened, and all the tools scattered and got back to their places as Sam walked back into the garage. He walked over to his new tool and picked it up and turned it on.

He reached back into the bag and pulled out a small box that had the word "accessories" written across on it. Sam placed this box down on the counter and opened it up.

One by one, Sam started to attach the accessories to the new tool.

This new tool was a multipurpose tool; it was smaller than anything in there, except the screwdrivers, and had more attachments than any other tool in the garage as well, and more than all the other tools put together.

This tool was so ergonomically correct in its design that wherever Sam placed his hand there were multiple indents so that his fingers could get a grip on this tool.

It was about 12 inches long, and it weighed twelve pounds.

As Sam turned it on to demonstrate the various things it could do, he was again like a kid playing with his new toy, trying to see all the cool stuff he could do with it.

Although small, its accessories included a vacuum, a drill, a small sander, shovel, a brush, and a little blade for cutting.

Sam stood there and looked at the new tool and said, "Next week, you and I are going to build my treehouse, and you are going to be the only thing I will need to do this."

He set the tool down on the counter but placed a towel under it as if it were his prized piece and the table was soiled. He then turned and walked out the garage again, leaving the tool on the countertop.

The tool sat there for a second, then opened its eyes, smiled at the other tools and said, "Hi, how are you? My name is Will. It is short for William, and just like my ancestors, I am here to conquer all tasks great and small." He then opened his arms wide and said, "I am the future," as all the other tools looked at him and smiled. No one could figure out just where he came from and who his ancestors were, or who was he a part of.

Dae looked at him and said, "You know, we are not sure where you came from, but I think at one point you were what society calls multicultural. At one point you were a part of all of us, and you will be part of us for the rest of our lives."

The funny thing was that no one felt threatened like they were going to be replaced by this new tool. Perhaps it was a combination of knowing they fully expected a new tool to come along sooner or later, and now that they got one, it seemed as though it was a part of all of them, one they could all relate to, and it was better to have it sooner than later.

They all walked over and shook the hands of the new tool and welcomed him into their world.

"The beautiful thing about a multicultural society is that it is a multi-purpose society," Dae said, "you represent the best of all of us, and together we all will grow as one."

CPSIA information can be obtained
at www.ICGtesting.com
Printed in the USA
BVHW031400281119
565099BV00005B/19/P